I0619356

PIRANTULAS

MICHAEL YOWELL

SEVERED PRESS
HOBART TASMANIA

PIRANTULAS

www.facebook.com/MichaelYowell
michaelyowellhorror@gmail.com

CHAPTER 1

The moonlight danced on the rolling surface of the Amazon River. This was a good night to do this. The sky was clear and the moon was full, which would aid Monique Washington in navigating to her destination.

She was edgy. Despite her wanting this desperately, she was still afraid. What if she was caught? Her career would be finished, and her employer would be shamed irreparably. But this was too important; tonight she would uncover the truth.

The boat Monique had purchased was adequate. It was in very good shape, even though it looked like a rust bucket. She had no doubt that it would get her to where she needed to go, and do it quietly. The boat's outboard motor was a two-stroke engine with a silent propeller. It was quiet enough—at low speed—that it could not be heard over the orchestra of crickets and frogs.

She piloted the boat for hours, continuing up the calm, vast river. Her GPS guided her to the area she had programmed in.

Eventually she arrived at the tributary she was told about. She steered the boat in, lowering her speed. Sensing she was close, she shut the motor off and paddled the rest of the way.

Monique saw it. There, against the starry backdrop of sky, was the silhouette of a building.

That's it, she thought.

She rowed to shore. When the hull was parked in the sediment, Monique stepped out of the boat. She made sure she had all the equipment she would need, especially her camera. Then she carefully entered the foliage and made her way toward the building.

Owls were heard. A jaguar called in the distance. Bamboo rats were very vocal. The sounds of fluttering, rustling leaves were all over, likely from small rodents running around at night.

Monique reached the secret research facility. She got to the steel fire exit door at the bottom of the three-story building, where she was told to be at midnight. Looking at her watch, she was glad she'd started her journey early tonight; otherwise she would've missed her window. But, as it worked out, she was right on time.

Now she just had to wait.

She heard more jungle noises. The rustling was more active, which her nerves took note of.

Monique was startled by the sound of a solid latch releasing. The door was unlocked and opened, quietly. A South American woman was in the doorway.

Rosa, Monique acknowledged.

Rosa, the facility's housekeeper and cook, was contacted by Monique through social media. Monique had little trouble bribing her to do this. Her employer's pockets were deep.

"Did you remember to disable the security cameras?" Monique whispered.

The housekeeper nodded. "*Sim*, I turn them off."

"No dogs, right?"

"No dogs. Just, please hurry, Miss."

Monique slipped inside and Rosa shut the door.

"Okay, listen," said Rosa, keeping her voice as low as possible. "The labs are that way, down the hall. I go now, I should be upstairs."

"All right. Thank you, Rosa."

"Remember, I can only leave the cameras off for thirty minutes. Then I must switch them back on."

That was more time than Monique would need. "No problem. Thanks again. I'll show myself out before then."

The housekeeper smiled, then turned and crept up the staircase.

Monique turned her flashlight on and moved stealthily down the hallway. She was worked up; this operation had been weeks in planning, and now she was finally carrying it out. Tonight she would discover what the billionaire Felix Strohm was working on. Her employer, Strohm's biggest competitor, had gotten wind that it was something very big and top secret. Then, when Strohm had left the States and brought his project all the way to the Amazon, they knew it was something they needed to get their hands on.

Monique saw two laboratories at the end of the hall, one on each side. She pushed open the door to one of the labs and entered. Using her flashlight, she looked for a file cabinet. Then, after seeing microscopes, flasks, beakers, pipettes, and analyzing equipment, she spotted a tall cabinet in the far corner.

Along the way, her attention was drawn to a large tank against a wall. It was the size of an above-ground swimming pool. She aimed her light at the water, but it was too murky for anything to be seen. Monique leaned closer to try to see what was being kept in the water.

She was pushed in from behind.

She fell headlong into the water, yelping before going under.

All of a sudden, the water was alive with frenzied activity. It felt like her body was being bumped and nudged all over. Whatever was in there was all around her.

Monique struggled to get to the edge of the tank. The things in the water continued to poke her. The water around her grew warm. She found herself suddenly drained of energy.

The last thing she saw before she lost consciousness was Rosa being thrown angrily into the tank with her.

Five minutes later, only their skeletons remained.

CHAPTER 2

The drone of the airplane's jets was somehow comforting. The plane had been in the air for an hour now, having departed from Orlando, and had another eight hours to go. Four passengers were on board the Gulfstream G550, cruising over the Atlantic Ocean toward South America.

"Felix Strohm," Brooke muttered, still in awe of the assignment she'd received.

"Come on, girl," the young woman across the aisle said. "It's no big deal. He's only, like, one of the richest men in the whole world."

The sarcasm brought a smile to Brooke's face. "Right?"

"I'm Brandi," the woman offered with a grin. She brushed her straightened hair aside, and Brooke admired her pretty cocoa skin. "Brandi Laurier. I just graduated from Harvard."

"What is your field?" said Brooke.

"Biomedical engineering," Brandi replied, "with an emphasis on genetics."

"Interesting. I'm Brooke Dempsey. Just got out of Columbia University with a chemical and physical biology degree."

"We must be working on some kind of genetic research," Brandi concluded.

"To be honest, I don't know *what* we're doing," said Brooke. "The packet was very vague."

"Mine too. But when I saw the letterhead, read the proposal for the chance to work for Felix Strohm, and saw the advance check, I couldn't pass it up."

"Me neither. What an opportunity. Even if we don't know what it is yet."

The two young men several rows in front of them were chatting and giggling. They had done so since boarding the plane. Clearly, they knew each other.

"Excuse me," Brandi called out. "Hey guys."

The fellows turned around. One had buzz-cut blond hair and a matching goatee. The other was taller, lean, and had medium-length dark-brown hair that was styled back neatly. This was the first time Brooke had gotten a clear view of their entire faces, and the taller one really caught her eye.

God, he's cute.

"Yo," said the blond man. "How're you ladies doing?"

"Good," Brandi said. "We were just talking about this—um, did you both get a package from—"

"Felix Strohm?"

"Yes."

They nodded. "Sure did," said the brunet.

"Okay. So, we're trying to figure out exactly what sort of research we're going to be doing down there. Do you have any idea?"

"Not really, no," said the blond. "But who cares? It's Felix Strohm! Plus, we'll be in the heart of the Amazon. Man, this is gonna be so cool."

"Are you both recent graduates as well?" asked Brooke.

The taller man locked eyes with her. He liked what he saw. The young lady's wavy brown hair draped—almost regally—down her front. And her hazel eyes were bright, striking.

"Yes," he said, keeping his focus. "We both just graduated from Swarthmore College. I have a degree in chemistry, and Stu here degreed in neuroscience."

"Okay," said Brandi. "It seems we're all scientists. I'm Brandi. Brandi Laurier, fresh out of Harvard."

"Hi. I'm Stuart Bantry. Call me Stu."

"And I'm Chance Lemenson," the brunet added.

Brooke looked directly at him. *Especially nice to meet you, Chance.* "I'm Brooke Dempsey."

The two shared an innocent smile. It was nothing but cordial, but it felt nicer than that.

"So, none of us really know anything about this project?" Brandi asked. "I mean, other than what the packet and contract said?"

They shrugged to each other and shook their heads.

"It must be something pretty sensitive," said Brooke.

Stuart frowned. "What do you mean?"

"Well, think about it. Felix Strohm's one of the richest men on the planet. He can afford the best of the best. Why does he bring *us* in? Total unknowns, with no field experience?"

Chance contemplated that. "I dunno. Maybe it's something that he can't trust to people who are already in the public eye."

"That's what bothers me."

"Look," said Stuart. "It's not like we're going to disappear there. It's not gonna be some scary, terrible Nazi-experiment thing."

Brandi raised an eyebrow. "Are you sure? I mean, look at us. We have a biomedical engineer, a chemical and physical biologist, a chemist, and a neuroscientist. That's exactly the kind of team needed to create some terrible Nazi experiment thing."

"We're probably going to be making some radioactive Creature from the Black Lagoon with twenty tentacles," said Chance.

Brandi snickered. "All that's missing is a paleontologist."

Brooke chuckled. "Don't worry, he probably has one there already."

The group laughed, enjoying the moment.

It did not take long for the four to build camaraderie. They talked about whatever crossed their minds, from school, to where they were from, to what they were going to do with the money from this assignment. The group got to know each other pretty well while the plane took them to Brazil.

CHAPTER 3

The jet touched down at Manau International Airport. After nine hours of flying, the passengers were eager to walk around on solid ground. The plane reached its private hangar and parked. The door was opened and everybody disembarked down the steps.

While waiting for their luggage, the travelers walked to the hangar entrance and stopped just outside. They breathed in the thick humidity and studied their surroundings, seeing the vast city of Manaus all around them.

"Here we are," beamed Stuart. "We're actually in Brazil."

"Yep," said Chance. "We're in Brazil, buddy." He stepped away from the others. Now that he was off the plane, he could finally have a cigarette. He pulled one from his pack and lit it. The first draw was a long one.

"Ew," Brandi whispered. "He smokes. Who does that anymore?"

Brooke didn't mind. "Doesn't bother me. I used to be a smoker."

Brandi grinned. She could see that there was probably nothing the young man could do that would bother Brooke.

Brooke walked over to join Chance. He instinctively held the cigarette away, so that its smoke wouldn't waft to her.

"Long flight, huh?" she said.

"For sure," Chance replied. "But well worth it. Visiting the Amazon is a bucket-list thing for a lot of people. And here we are, doing it in our twenties." He took another puff. When he exhaled, the breeze carried the smoke directly to Brooke.

"Oh shit, I'm sorry," he said.

"Don't worry about it," Brooke eased. "I'm not one of those preachy people. I used to smoke, myself."

That made him feel better.

A few minutes later, a black Lincoln Navigator pulled up to the hangar. Its driver, a tall man with a dark complexion, stepped out of the SUV and addressed the group.

"Greetings," he said, leaving his sunglasses on. "I'm Benny, and I've been sent by Mr. Strohm to take you all to your hotel."

"Great," said Stuart. He carried his luggage to the SUV, where the driver took it and placed it in the back of the vehicle.

The driver then put everybody else's belongings inside with Stuart's. He shut the liftgate and turned to the group. "Shall we?"

"Yes sir," said Chance. He ducked inside the Lincoln, and Brooke and Brandi followed. Stuart sat in the front passenger seat. Everything packed and everybody loaded, the driver started the engine and pulled away from the hangar.

The car took them out of Manaus, across the Rio Negro, and west toward the jungle. Much of the scenery looked like that of Florida side roads, but the farther they drove, the more the terrain resembled that of Hawaii. Then Mexico. They drove past tiny eateries and through small towns. Then, after a while, there was nothing but a few scattered homes here and there along the narrow highway.

Finally, they arrived in Manacapuru, a sizable city at the edge of the Amazon River. The driver brought them all the way through the city and to a small hotel right on the river. He parked there and got out to retrieve his passengers' belongings from the back.

The sun had set, leaving a beautiful palate of orange and pink in the western sky. It was made more stunning by showing its reflection in the vast river.

"God, look at that," said Brooke.

"So pretty," Brandi said, taking a few quick pictures.

Stuart saw an indoor/outdoor restaurant and bar at the far side of the hotel. "Hey, guys. Let's get situated, and then meet over there for some dinner and some drinks."

"Amen," said Chance. "I could go for some food."

The group got checked into their reserved rooms. After freshening up, they met again at the bar. The menu contained dishes that were unknown to them, so they played it safe and ordered what looked the most familiar; steak and fried fish dinners. The hungry visitors ate until they were full and washed the food down with cold beer.

"Here we are," said Chance, raising his bottle. "To us, and our mysterious work in the jungle."

"Hear hear," Stuart followed, and they all toasted.

Chance emptied his bottle. "I need another beer," he said. "Anyone else?"

Stuart's was half full. "Not yet."

The ladies shook their heads, good for the time being.

"Remember," Brooke prompted, "we have to be at the dock by eight a.m."

Chance rolled his eyes. "I know, I know. We'll be fine." He got up from the table and strolled toward the bar.

Brooke watched him walk away. *Nice butt*, she thought.

Seeing that other patrons were smoking inside, Chance wanted to as well. He reached into his pocket and pulled a cigarette from its pack. Then he stopped to light it.

A hand reached in from out of nowhere and plucked the cigarette from his mouth.

What the fuck?

Chance followed it, turning his head. He saw a young Asian man. Lean, taut, with his chest pushed out. The man gave a smug grin, turned around, and took a seat at his table of friends.

"Look, man," Chance began. But before he could step up, another man wedged himself between them.

"You should walk away, please," the stranger said. His accent was one Chance couldn't place. The man's hair and skin were almost caramel colored.

"Why?"

"That's—just how he is. It's his way of mingling with people."

Chance held back a laugh. "Seriously?"

"Come on, I'll buy you a drink, yes?"

Chance shrugged. "Sure. We'll take it outside." Then he leaned his head and made his voice loud enough for the Asian to hear. "Where I can smoke."

The stranger brought Chance to the bartender, paid for what Chance ordered, and escorted him to the deck outside. There was a nice view of the river from there, and it calmed Chance. He lit a cigarette and smoked it while taking in the sight.

"Again, I am sorry for him," said the caramel-toned man. "Please, enjoy your night." And with that, the man excused himself and vanished inside the bar.

It only took three minutes for Chance to be visited again. Seeing someone approach from the corner of his eye, he looked to see the cocky Asian walking toward him.

Oh man, he thought.

Chance kept his eyes fixed on the man. The man came right up to him. Chance felt his heart beat faster. He didn't want any trouble—God forbid something happened that would land him in a Brazilian jail—but at the same time, he was the type of person who stood his ground.

"Whatcha doing here, *gae*?" the man said.

Chance took another drag of his cigarette. "Smoking, bro."

"I mean, whatcha doing here in my town?"

"Came for the sights," Chance smirked.

The man brought his face closer to Chance's cigarette. "What do you plan on doing with your cigarette butt when you're finished?"

Despite his urge to give a nasty reply, Chance stayed silent. His adrenaline was pumping.

"Are you gonna put it in my nice river?"

"You ask a lot of fucking questions," said Chance, with no timidity in his swelling voice.

The man felt it. He knew he had pushed as far as he should; he could tell that this guy was one step away from a full-on fight.

"I do," the man admitted, holding up his hands. "But I like your answers."

The hint of a smile crept up the side of Chance's mouth.

"My name is Danny. Danny Kim."

Chance didn't care.

"Okay, okay. I'm sorry for behaving like I did." He extended a hand.

"Yeah?"

"Yeah."

Chance took his hand and shook it in forgiveness. "I'm Chance Lemenson, from the States."

Danny nodded. "What brings you to the jungle, Mr. Chance?"

Hesitation set in. Chance wondered what he should say about why he and his companions were here in Brazil. He knew the project was a secret.

"No reason," he finally said. "Just wanted to see the Amazon with my friends."

"Ah. And here I thought you were going to be part of Mr. Strohm's new research team."

Chance was stunned. "Hold on. You knew about that?"

"I knew someone was coming. I am to take four Americans upriver tomorrow morning."

"Wait, so you're—"

"The boat captain," Danny stated. His chest stuck out when he said it.

Brooke came out to the deck to make sure Chance was okay. She had seen the Asian bothering him, and she wanted to help him if she could.

"Hi," she said, taking in the air. "Some night, huh?"

"It's very cool being here," Chance responded. "Brooke, meet Danny. He's our boat captain for tomorrow."

"Oh!" She hadn't expected that. "That's great. Nice to meet you, Danny."

"You too," Danny said. He directed his attention back to Chance. "I'll see the four of you at the dock tomorrow morning, right down there."

They followed his finger to a sturdy but weathered river boat moored to the small pier.

"Eight a.m.," Brooke confirmed.

The captain walked away, leaving the American couple to themselves.

"That was weird," said Chance.

"What happened? It looked like he was going to pick a fight."

"That's what I thought, too. But he wasn't. Guess he just likes to see people's reactions, or something like that." He took a swig of beer.

"Okay…I'd watch out for him. He seems to have behavioral issues that might be serious."

Chance shooed the air. "Meh. All he has to do is get us to Mr. Strohm. After that, I'm sure we'll never see him again."

CHAPTER 4

The group met at the pier the following morning. Their boat captain, Danny Kim, was waiting there, as was the man with the caramel hair and peculiar accent from last night. They had a large haul of food and supplies next to them, undoubtedly to be delivered to Felix Strohm.

"Good morning," the copper-toned man said. "My name is Guaré Begu, and some of you have already met Captain Danny Kim. I'm the first mate."

The passengers introduced themselves. When that was finished, the captain invited everybody aboard. They loaded their belongings and took seats where they could on the boat. Danny and his mate stowed the consignment of food and supplies. Then Danny went to the wheelhouse, started the engine, and pulled his forty-foot river boat away from the pier.

They started their journey southwest on the Amazon River. It seemed more like a lake than a river. The travelers were in awe of its size. The river was two miles wide.

"I can't believe how wide it is," Brooke marveled.

"I can't believe how brown the water is," said Stuart.

"Well, there's a lot of flow in a river this size," Brandi explained. "That means a lot of sediment with it. Have you ever seen the Mississippi River?"

Stuart shook his head.

"Same thing. A big, powerful river, brown with muddy sediment."

Brooke's eyes wandered across the vast water. She spotted something gently breaching the water. It was a long, narrow snout with visible teeth. *What is that?* Then the rest of the head surfaced, and it looked like a dolphin with pink skin.

"That's a pink river dolphin!" Brooke said excitedly. "I've always wanted to see one. There should be manatees in these waters, too."

"Yes," said Guaré. "Dolphins, manatees, anacondas, caimans, giant otters, and thousands of different fish."

"What kinds of wildlife on land?" asked Chance.

"Oh, let me think. We have jaguars, capybaras, tapirs, sloths, and many types of monkeys."

"And other wonderful jungle things, I'm sure," said Stuart, sarcastically. "Like snakes, spiders, and bats."

The captain looked back from the wheelhouse, chuckling. "Of course. Some of the largest around." He stuck his chest out and smacked it.

"And if you see any pretty little frogs, don't touch them," Brooke warned. "They're poison dart frogs. The batrachotoxin on their skin can kill you."

Stuart gave a sarcastic thumbs-up. "Super."

"We didn't sign that disclaimer for nothing," said Chance.

The boat cruised up the river. It was a serene journey. The sun was bright, and the air warm. Lush green scenery treated their eyes. The shores were lined with palms, sorvas, and towering rubber trees.

There was a cacophony of noise from the birds of the surrounding jungle. The travelers heard a mixture of toucans, macaws, trogons, tinamous, and the extremely loud screaming pihas. Brooke loved every minute of it.

Hours later, they were deeper in the heart of the Amazon rainforest. The river was slightly narrower here, and the foliage thicker.

"Ah, here we are," said Guaré, recognizing the opening to their destination.

Danny slowed the engine and turned into a tributary. The waterway was only a hundred feet wide. As they entered, a howler monkey called out.

The terrifying sound caused Brooke to jump, as she was not expecting it.

Chance smiled, but he wasn't going to laugh at her. It had made him jump a little bit himself. "*Welcome to the jungle*," he sang.

She flashed him a wry smile.

The boat kept to the center of the channel and drove deeper into the rainforest. Troops of spider monkeys could be seen in the surrounding trees. Some were hanging from their tails and picking fruit, and some were chasing each other among the branches while barking playfully.

Then, from out of nowhere, the group saw a square concrete complex. It was three stories in height, with windows all around the second and third floors.

"You're home," Danny announced to his passengers. He veered toward a short pier and drifted in. Large balsa trees were on either side of the pier, their curtain-like buttresses rooted in the water. The captain eased up to the end of the pier, and Guaré moored the boat.

Everybody grabbed their things and began to file out onto the pier.

"Holy shit!" Stuart exclaimed from the rear. "What was that?"

The others looked. "What?" said Chance.

"There was something in the water, right by the boat, and it was huge!"

"Like an alligator?" Brandi said. "A black caiman?"

"No, like smooth and long. Like the biggest fish I've ever seen."

"Ah, likely a *pirarucu*," said Guaré. "They get as long as four meters in these waters."

"Holy shit," Stuart repeated, with a nervous laugh. "That's, like, thirteen feet."

Brooke felt humble. "Guess I won't be taking a swim anytime soon," she joked.

"You're not kidding," the captain said. "Some of these big fish will take a bite out of you. Plus, there are about a hundred species of electric fish and electric eel in the Amazon."

"Do not forget the piranha," added Guaré.

Brooke nodded. "Naturally. Most people *do* think about piranhas when they think Amazon River."

There was movement from the jungle, and everyone looked. Three men emerged from the foliage to meet them. The lead man smiled, creating wrinkles in his perfectly-tanned face. His guests instantly recognized him as the famed billionaire, Felix Strohm. He had fair hair, sparkling green eyes, and looked to be in his mid-forties. He was shorter than his cohorts, but he was quite fit.

"Welcome," he said. "I'm Felix Strohm, your host."

The group members said hello to him while they brought their belongings ashore. Strohm went to the boat captain and handed an envelope to him. Then Danny and his first mate steered away from the pier and left.

As Brooke watched the boat chug away, she felt—for the briefest of moments—the sense of abandonment.

"Please," said Strohm, "follow me." He and his staff members took hold of the food and supplies brought to them and walked into the trees.

The guests followed. Carrying their luggage, they stayed on the heels of their new associates. There was a clear path in the woods that was easy to navigate, leading directly to the complex. They walked uphill, around the building, and to the main entrance.

Strohm punched a code into the lock, and the door unlocked. "The code is two-four-six-eight," he announced to the guests. He brought them all inside and shut the door behind them. It was considerably cooler in the climate-controlled building.

"I'm Chance Lemenson," Chance said, starting the introductions. "This is a real honor, sir, to be working with you."

"The pleasure is mine, I'm sure."

The others presented themselves also.

"I'm Brandi Laurier, from Harvard University."

"Brooke Dempsey, chemical and physical biologist."

"Stuart. Stuart Bantry. Call me Stu."

"Very nice to meet you all in person," said Strohm. He turned to his left, facing a Latino man. "This is Manuel Diego, our zoologist. He comes to us from Houston."

The researchers greeted him with nods and smiles.

Strohm switched his attention to the other man. "And finally, this is Hans Pichler. He's our paleontologist."

"See?" Brooke whispered to Brandi, grinning. "I told you so."

Brandi stifled a giggle, remembering Brooke's joke about how Strohm probably had a paleontologist.

"Lovely to meet you all," said Hans. "I look forward to us working together."

"Leave your things here by the door," said Strohm. "We'll get them later. Would you all like to see around?"

They nodded as one, eager to see the facility.

Strohm took them through, showing the researchers where everything was. The main floor was the living area, with a recreation room, a utility room, a dining room, and an open kitchen. The top floor was for lodging; there were eight bedrooms of equal size, each with a window and an attached bathroom.

Then they went to the bottom floor. "This is where the labs are; where the magic happens," said Strohm, eliciting a chuckle from the group. There were two separate laboratories, containing subject tanks, terrariums, and all the equipment the researchers could hope for.

"You have a very impressive facility, Mr. Strohm," said Brandi. She was excited to use some of the equipment.

"Come, everybody," said Strohm. "Dinner should be ready soon. I hope you're hungry."

"I'm starved," Stuart admitted. The prospect of dinner was sheer delight.

The tour complete, Strohm led everybody back up the stairs to the main floor. He had them take their belongings up to their new rooms and freshen up if they needed to. Then they all convened at the dining table.

The table was dark mahogany, with a seal of urethane, surrounded by wrought-iron chairs. The dinner plates were already set. Everybody filtered into the chairs and took their seats.

Strohm held his hand out to introduce his new cook. "This is Oscar, our chef. Tonight he has chosen to make you a traditional meal to welcome you to the Amazon."

The cook nodded to all, and began serving his soup. It was *tacacá*, a pungent shrimp soup.

The guests ate. Strohm was entertained by their facial expressions as they tried the sour, spicy, acidic flavor for the first time.

Oscar then brought out their entrées. The main course was a local fish, seared and basted, served with greens in a yellow sauce. The graduates dug in, really enjoying this evening's culinary surprises.

"This is delicious, Mr. Strohm," said Stuart. "What is it?"

"It's jaraqui. One of the abundant fish in the region."

"It is prepared with salt, lemon, and *cheiro verde*," the cook, Oscar, informed. "Then it is topped with *tucupí* sauce. The sauce alone takes several days to ferment, boil, and cook perfectly. The wild yuca juice is what gives it its yellow color."

"Well, sir," said Chance, "it's delicious. Bravo."

Oscar beamed proudly and gave a thankful bow. Then he retreated to the kitchen so the group could enjoy their meal.

After the lavish dinner, everybody relaxed with more table conversation.

"Mr. Strohm," said Stuart, "what made you decide to build your facility here, in the middle of the jungle?"

"Two reasons," their employer stated. "First, many of the specimens we will be working with are native species abundant to the area."

"Which species?" asked Brooke.

"River life, mostly. Piranha and lungfish. And some legged predators."

"Cool," said Stuart.

"And the second reason?" said Chance.

A sly smile crept up one side of Strohm's face. "Taxes."

The table shared a chuckle.

"So, tonight," Strohm said, "I would like you all to relax, unwind, rest, sleep. Enjoy your first night here." He raised his water glass halfway. "Tomorrow, we start working."

CHAPTER 5

Everybody gathered at the table the next morning for coffee and breakfast. After their hot meal, Strohm stood up from his chair at the end of the table.

"I suppose you're all wondering what you're here for," he said, almost teasingly.

"Um, yes," said Brandi. "We've been dying to find out."

"Okay." Strohm cleared his throat. "The four of you have been selected by me because of your academic achievements. You're each in the top five percentile of your fields of study. What I want to do is something groundbreaking. I want us to pioneer the field of genetic therapy."

Stuart was interested. "Oh?" was all he said.

"What kind of therapy?" asked Brandi.

"Eventually, anything. The first stage of our research is to figure out how to successfully augment animals' physical characteristics without having to wait for generational adaptation. The second stage will be to use the procedure to treat diseases in animals. And then, the third stage will be human trials. Curing terminal diseases and healing the crippled would be as simple as performing an operation—a transplant."

"Regenerative medicine," Brandi acknowledged, mostly to herself.

"Wow," said Chance. "That's a fascinating proposal."

"It sure is," Stuart seconded. "I'm in a daze right now, trying to take it all in."

Strohm laughed reassuringly. "Don't worry, I don't expect you to, upon first hearing. It's going to be a long road. But when it's over, I promise that you will have helped change the world."

Eager to begin, the group accompanied Felix Strohm down to the laboratories. They entered the one on the left side of the floor. Strohm flipped the lights on and led the others to a steel tank along one wall. It looked like a long, narrow above-ground swimming pool. White PVC pipes were attached to both ends, continuously pumping water through.

"This is one of the specimens we will focus on," said Strohm.

Looking in, the researchers saw a massive school of fish, each one about twelve inches long.

"There are over fifty different species of piranha," said Manuel. "The red-bellied piranha—

Pygocentrus nattereri—has the strongest jaws and sharpest teeth. The locals call them *navalha*—the razor."

"Is that what these are?" Stuart asked.

"Yes."

"The razor," Chance repeated softly, studying their protruding lower jaws.

"They're pretty," Brooke remarked. She looked closer to examine their teeth. They were sizable white triangles, making the jaw look like the edge of a saw blade. She could imagine the damage those razor-sharp teeth could do.

"The red-bellied are the most aggressive and most dangerous of them all," the zoologist continued. "When they feed, they spread out in search of prey. Then, when one of them finds prey, it signals the others. They come fast and furious. Their bites are strong, quick, and clean. In fact, people who have been bitten by them often don't even know they've been bitten until they see the blood in the water around them."

"Yikes," said Stuart.

Chance leaned forward. "Is that a *bone* in there?"

Strom felt a surge of panic. He thought he had removed all of the skeletal remains in the tank. Quickly, he smiled.

"They must be fed," he stated. "Sometimes I'll treat them to a leg of capybara."

Cool, thought Stuart. He would like to see a feeding.

"One of nature's perfect predators," Strohm continued. "We're going to try to enhance them, to see if we can improve their state."

Brooke frowned. "Enhance them?"

The billionaire nodded. "Yes. We've already begun introducing steroids into their systems. That is part of the first stage of our research. From there, we'll get more creative. Remember, the goal is to be able to genetically enhance and repair cells. Humans, eventually."

Stuart was excited about the potential. He was starting to understand the need for neuroscientists, biologists, and chemists to be working together on this project.

"Come," said Strohm, "let's introduce you to the other specimens."

They migrated to the lab across the hall. Once inside, they were brought to the large glass terrarium there. Scanning the recreated jungle inside, the group saw six gigantic tarantulas, brown with black and brown barbed hairs. They were the largest tarantulas the graduates had ever seen.

"Holy smokes," said Brandi. "I've never seen one this big."

"These are *Theraphosa blondi*, or the Goliath birdeater," said Manuel.

Chance couldn't help but grin.

"The Amazon tarantula can reach a size of thirteen inches across," Manuel informed.

Brooke shuddered at the thought. "Wow. That's like the size of a giant huntsman spider."

"And," Hans added, "the tarantula has been around since the Cretaceous period. A hundred-and-twenty million years ago. Like sharks, they have remained essentially the same their entire existence."

"They're poisonous, aren't they?" said Chance.

Brandi rolled her hand side to side. "Yes, technically, but their venom is too weak to really affect humans. Their bite usually feels no worse than a wasp sting."

"Be mindful of their hairs," said Manuel. "They can embed and irritate the skin. Wear nitrile gloves when handling them."

"So, here's how I want to proceed," Strohm announced. "Miss Dempsey and Mr. Bantry, I'd like you and Hans to start with the piranhas. Mr. Lemenson, Miss Laurier, and Manuel will begin with the tarantulas."

Brooke was disappointed that she was paired with Stuart instead of Chance. "You're splitting us up?" she said. "We're not all working together?"

Strohm chuckled. "No, that's not it. Of course I want you all to collaborate and share data. Feel free to move from lab to lab. But since we have two very different test species, I would like the focus to be equal on both. That way, our progress on both will be simultaneous."

Chance nodded. "Makes sense."

"All right," said Strohm, clapping his hands together. "Let's get started."

CHAPTER 6

The subsequent weeks were arduous and frustrating. Stressful. Mentally punishing.

The group of researchers performed transplant experiments. They were to take fins from one fish and attach them to another fish. At the same time, they worked on surgically adding legs from one spider to another.

Brooke's mastery of biology and Stuart's training in neuroscience were key to the success of the first experiments. Manuel's zoological advice was taken into consideration as well.

Hans Pichler, the paleontologist, was also a gifted surgeon. He used to practice in Lithuania. Paleontology was always his passion, though. He was fascinated by the evolutions of extinct species. When asked to join Felix Strohm's staff, Hans was pleased that the billionaire was hiring him for both his surgery skills and his paleontology knowledge.

Chance developed an injection that would temporarily put the fish into a state of suspended animation in order for it to survive being out of the water while it was being experimented on. Hans and Stuart performed most of the surgical duties, while Brandi and Brooke lent a hand when they could. Chance and Manuel assisted however they could, but for the most part, they observed.

Eventually, the group managed to successfully transplant functioning pectoral fins to the musculature of one of the piranhas. Releasing it back into its tank, they were fascinated watching the fish figure out its modified body. It learned how to swim faster with its new fins.

They were triumphant in the other lab as well. An additional pair of legs was integrated into one of the tarantulas' cephalothorax. It did not take long for the spider to adapt, and it was soon quicker and more agile than ever before.

Now that the procedures had been effectively completed, the research team proudly studied their work. What they had accomplished was incredible.

*   *   *

"Now for a true challenge," Strohm presented to the group. "We are going to attempt to add the lungs from a lungfish to the piranha."

"What?" said Chance. "Is that even possible?"

Strohm shrugged. "I certainly hope so. I want to make the piranha have the ability to breathe out of the water."

Brooke felt an unexplained discomfort. "Why would you want to do that?"

"Remember our endgame," said Strohm. "If we want to someday cure people with the power of regenerative medicine, we need to push the boundaries. Find out exactly where our limits are."

"I suppose," she said. "But they are two completely different classes."

"I have faith in you all," Strohm emphasized.

"How are we going to link the different proteins?" asked Stuart.

"We'd need to introduce the separate DNA gradually," Brooke said.

"Maybe a chemical agent that will aid in the molecular adhesion," said Strohm.

Chance rubbed his chin. "That might help. Something to interpret the genetic code from one species to the other."

"Yes! A genetic interpreter…I like that."

"Do you have any ideas?" asked Stuart.

"Eh. Not really, but if I was going to start, I'd base something in sodium and potassium."

Brooke agreed. "Good idea. That's a friendly environment for forming enzymes."

The billionaire was excited by the group's enthusiasm. "Fantastic!" he said, clapping his hands together. "I can't wait for us to get started."

*   *   *

Chance created several formulas in which the cells could chemically bond, but his first six failed. Finally, the seventh formula held up to the tests. Chance eagerly made it into a serum.

The researchers spent another two weeks operating on piranhas and lungfish. Several subjects died during the experiments. But the team would not give up.

The procedure was obviously a difficult one. Thanks to Chance's new serum, however, the tissues of the two animals accepted each other. The placement of the lung inside the piranha was the hardest part. It took some major surgery to connect the main airway and the blood vessels.

More test subjects died. This was to be expected. The group was not deterred; they kept trying.

Finally, one of the subjects survived the operation. The researchers were elated with their success. They studied the fish as it acclimated using its lung for oxygen. It was fantastic to watch.

*   *   *

"Next," said Strohm, "we're going to proceed to a new challenge. We will attempt to transplant limbs and organs from one phylum's animal to another's."

The paleontologist smiled. He had anticipated this news, and he was fascinated by the idea.

Stuart raised his head. "What exactly are we going to try to do?"

Strohm cleared his throat. "We are going to transplant the head of a piranha onto the body of a tarantula."

Chance wasn't sure he'd heard right. "What?"

Strohm nodded, grinning. "That's right. The head of a piranha onto the body of a tarantula."

"That's going to require some serious tissue engineering," stated Brandi.

Stuart took a deep breath. As the neuroscientist, this was where he would be needed the most. He would have to attach the brain and nervous system to the tarantula's anatomy. Nothing like this had ever been done before.

"A piranha's head is much larger than that of a tarantula," said Brooke. "Our best chance would be to use the smaller fish and the biggest tarantulas."

Stuart agreed. "Naturally. Keep the physiological scale relative."

"I'm glad each one of you is here to help me make history," Strohm said. "The scientific advances our work will introduce are limitless."

"Most definitely," said Hans. "It could even lead to a cure for cancer."

Brandi raised her hand timidly, as if she were back in school. "I understand what we're all doing here, but why exactly have you chosen to put a piranha head on a tarantula?"

Strohm looked her directly in the eye. "My goal is to marry the two species into one apex animal."

*   *   *

Chance stood at the rail of the balcony and lit a cigarette. There was time for a smoke before dinner. It was early evening, and the jungle was still hot and steamy. At least there was a little breeze hitting his side of the building.

Brooke opened the door and stepped out to join Chance. He smiled when he saw her.

"Some day, huh?" he said.

"Oh yes," Brooke replied. "Just when you thought you'd heard it all, right?"

He chuckled. "I know, right? Oh my God…we're making an abomination of nature."

"I'm still trying to wrap my brain around it," said Brooke. "Why would somebody be devoting this much time and money to intentionally create an animal like that?"

"I'm sure it's not because he likes exotic pets."

"Do you think maybe…? I dunno, but maybe he's working for the government or something? Like, hired to create a superpredator that could be used in war? Some kind of bioweapon?"

Chance laughed. "You've seen too many movies."

"What, then?" Brooke presented. "Because it certainly can't be something that is being made to benefit its ecosystem."

Chance nodded. "That's true. If this new species were ever released into the ecosystem, it would totally alter it. Maybe destroy it."

"Right."

Chance thought about it for a moment. Then he turned to face Brooke and said, "God, you may not be wrong about the bioweapon theory."

There was a *creak* behind them.

Jolted, they turned to look back. The breeze was tickling an outdoor thermometer, causing it to sway on its rusty metal hook.

False alarm, thought Brooke. She leaned closer to Chance and said, "I think we'd be smart to not talk about such things out loud around here."

CHAPTER 7

Early one morning, Brooke got out of bed and prepared to go down to the kitchen for some coffee on the balcony. When she opened her door, she caught sight of Stuart leaving Brandi's room. He went stealthily to his own room and shut himself inside.

Well, what do you know? thought Brooke.

A moment later, Brandi emerged from her room. She shut the door and began down the hallway toward Brooke. Judging by the sly grin on Brooke's face, Brandi was sure Stuart was seen leaving her room.

"Mornin', girl," said Brandi.

"Morning. So…you and Stu, huh?"

Brandi was not ashamed. "A girl's gotta get some action once in a while, know what I'm sayin'?"

"I guess so," Brooke said. "How did you—when—what made the two of you—"

"Do it?"

"Yeah."

"Like naughty freaks all night long?"

Brooke giggled. "Yeah."

"Well," Brandi explained, "this girl has needs. I've been eyeing that boy for the last week or so. Then, last night, I asked him to come to my room so we could talk. One thing led to another—I made sure of that—and we did it. It was fantastic. Plus, I like him. He's funny."

"I think that's great."

"So, are you hooking up with Chance yet?"

Brooke was taken aback. "What? No...why would you think that?"

Brandi smirked. "Come on. It's obvious you're into him."

"Oh? Obvious?"

"Yep."

Brooke wasn't going to lie. "Okay, I do have a thing for him. But I don't think he feels the same way. He hasn't made a single move on me."

"Then maybe *you* should."

The thought made Brooke nervous. "Me?"

"Um-hmm. Some guys are too shy; you have to make the first move."

"I don't know. I'd be mortified if I did something like that and he were to shoot me down."

"Shit," Brandi scoffed. "This isn't high school. You're a grown woman. And a pretty one at that. You should be secure enough with yourself whether he wants you or not."

"You're right."

"Besides, I watch Chance sometimes. He checks you out, you know."

Brooke felt a little jolt run through her body. "Really?"

"Yep. Don't worry, girl, he's into you. Make a move."

"All right. Now come on, let's go down and get some coffee."

*　　*　　*

Early that evening, after a hearty and healthy dinner, Chance prepared to go out to the balcony for a cigarette. Before he reached the sliding glass door, Brooke nudged his arm.

"You want to take a walk down to the pier?" she asked him.

It was a nice evening, and relaxing by the river would be nice. Especially with someone to talk to.

"Sure," he said.

Brooke could tell by the smile on his face that he genuinely liked the idea. She was excited – today would be the day she would try to make her move.

The two of them left the building, rounded the corner, and walked downhill through the path in the jungle. A few minutes later, the shoreline and wooden pier were in view. The couple strolled to the end of the pier and sat down.

While they chatted, they took notice of the jungle around them. They watched the monkeys in the tree. They listened to birdsong. Then, from somewhere on the water, what sounded like a raspy cough was heard.

"What was that?" said Chance. "I've been hearing that every once in a while, whenever I'm outside."

Brooke looked out across the water. Then something breached the surface and made the same sound. Upon seeing it, she realized what it was.

"That's that *pirarucu*," she said. "You know, that huge thing Stu saw in the water when we first got here."

"Oh yeah, the—um—arapaima. With the giant scales."

"Uh huh."

"That's what we ate that one night in Oscar's fish stew with the palm oil."

"Remember when Manuel told us about how it is air breathing?"

Chance nodded. "Yup, I do."

"And that when it comes up for breaths, it sounds like a cough when they gulp air."

He took a moment to admire the oddities of the Amazon. "That's so crazy," he finally said. "Nature has so many different methods of survival."

"I think it's cool," said Brooke. "Mother Nature is bound to no rules. I mean, air-breathing fish, bats using sonar, and squirrels with webbing to fly."

He chuckled. "Or tarantulas with piranha heads."

Brooke added fuel. "Does that make us 'Mother's little helpers'?"

Their eyes met while they laughed it out. Then the laughter subsided, but their eyes remained locked.

Her hazel eyes were bright, as if full of energy. They drew him in. Chance felt the moment, and he was about to lean in and—

"Kiss me," she said softly.

They brought their mouths together. Her lips were warm and soft. The kiss was gentle, sweet, nice. Chance felt a warmth in his chest.

The kiss grew stronger. His lips parted, allowing the tip of his tongue to be felt. Her tongue flirtatiously responded to his.

The pair took each other in their arms, their passion growing. Chance nuzzled her neck, kissing it, taking in the scent of her skin.

Before long, they were worked up; they had to stop. At least for now.

There was glee on both of their faces. Excitement. Happiness. They gazed into each other's eyes.

"Hi," Brooke whispered playfully.

"Hey, you," he replied. "That was really nice. I didn't think you liked me like that."

She simply nodded. "Later on, tonight, I'll show you how much I like you."

Chance's eyes lit up, as did a spark in his core. He smiled. "I'd have to say that's a totally terrific plan."

They decided it was time to rejoin the others. Holding hands, the couple walked up the path leading back to the complex.

CHAPTER 8

A few more weeks had gone by. The researchers had made steady progress.

Hans and Stuart had worked their skills in the surgical department, arduously piecing together tissue and tendon to attain the desired result. Chance's serum had acted as a genetic translator to foster the bond of the two species.

After several failed attempts, they had finally reconstructed a hybrid animal that survived the procedure.

"And," said Stuart, when the surgery was complete, "we have lift-off."

The group circled the unconscious creature and watched it breathe. The piranha mouth yawned for air, and the lungs of the arachnid took it in.

"This is so exciting!" said Hans. "Look at it!" He sounded like a father meeting his newborn child.

Yeah, look at it, thought Brandi with opposite enthusiasm. The creature was hideous. Its large red-tinted eyes were glazed in slumber, appearing to judge the people around it while its triangular teeth gleamed. The stitching was holding, keeping its head attached to the furry body.

"That is one ugly spider," Brooke remarked.

The others chuckled, unable to deny that fact.

"I see an issue with it," stated Manuel. "With a mouth that size, shouldn't it be able to move its head to help feed itself?"

The others pondered, then agreed that he had a point. The creature needed something of a neck in order to be more effective with its jaws against prey.

"We could lengthen the throat," suggested Stuart. "With some infused muscle tissue. Maybe from a small anaconda or something similar."

"Yes," said Strohm. "Perfect."

"Not much," warned Brooke, "or it will be too front-heavy. The spider weighs very little to begin with. Adding the fish's head will be challenging enough for the body to get used to."

"Agreed," Stuart said. "We'll keep the added tissue to a minimum. That would be easier on me, as well."

Hans nodded. "Me too."

"Okay," said Strohm. "Let's get the specimen isolated before it wakes up. We'll keep it alive, study it, and track its progress."

The group started moving the creature to its own glass tank.

"And tomorrow," said Strohm, "we'll start with the new enhancement."

*   *   *

Two more weeks of intensive work passed.

The inclusion of snake vertebra and muscle was successful. The creature now had a short one-inch neck, which would enable its head to move more freely.

The group stood above the specimen secured by straps to the operating table, and they admired their work.

"God, it's even uglier now," said Chance.

"You got that right," Brandi acknowledged.

"Now, now," Strohm said playfully. "Don't hurt his feelings. I think he's a beautiful work of art."

Everybody laughed. But despite its physical appearance, the creature's ugliness was eclipsed by the magnificence of its miraculous existence.

"I think I'll name him Boris," said Strohm.

Hans grimaced. "*Boris?*"

Strohm nodded emphatically. "Yeah…Boris. I like that."

The others didn't even want to ask why. After all, this was the billionaire's project, and he could name his property whatever he wanted.

"Hey, look," said Brandi, "he's coming to."

Chance frowned. "Already? He should be out for, like, another hour."

Sure enough, the animal was gaining consciousness. Its legs tucked and stretched, and the body began to wiggle.

Strohm was ecstatic. "That's it, Boris. Wake up and say hello."

Its eyes sharpened and aimed around the room. The creature quickly realized that it was in the presence of a threatening species. The hairs on its body seemed to bristle. It also noticed that it was bound to the table. It writhed spastically, trying to get free.

"Wow!" said Brooke. "Look at that energy...and he just woke up!"

The frustrated animal instinctively lashed out by biting the air. It bit with a pecking motion, made possible by the lengthening of its neck. The teeth could be heard gnashing together hard. It was becoming quite aggressive.

Stuart noticed one of its legs had wriggled free from the bottom strap. "Uh oh," he said.

"What?" said Brandi.

"His leg is...climbing."

Sure enough, the group saw that the creature's leg was above the lower strap and was pushing the body upward. Another leg slipped through, and the body flattened and squirmed loose of that strap.

"Shit," Stuart mumbled, not knowing what to do.

"Um…" Strohm looked around the lab for something in which to secure the animal. If only he had the steel specimen carrier he had originally captured the tarantulas with. But that piece of equipment was upstairs in the storage room. Then he decided to put the beast in the largest glass terrarium, the one with the other tarantula specimens, since it had a steel mesh cover that could be locked shut.

The creature was almost out of the top strap now.

"We have to grab him with something!" said Strohm. "Gotta get 'im in that case."

Chance's eyes darted. "With what?" He saw nothing they could use to safely carry the wild animal.

"Hurry!" cried Brandi, watching the animal squeeze free.

Chance ripped his lab coat off and smothered the creature with it. "Open the top!" he directed. Then, terrified of getting bitten through the fabric, he grabbed the mass and ran to the glass case.

Strohm got the top open just in time. He watched Chance empty the coat, and the creature was dumped into the case. Then Strohm quickly shut the steel-screen top and latched it.

"Holy shit," said Strohm, his heart pounding. He looked at the others and said, "Great job, everyone."

The rest of the group approached the case to see the animal react to its surroundings.

The creature scurried up the terrarium's foliage. It smacked into the cover, but the latch was secure. Insistent, it charged the mesh again. And again.

"I don't like this," said Brandi.

"It's okay," Strohm reassured.

Finally, the animal conceded. It crawled to the bottom and assessed its prison. Movement caught its keen eye. One of the other tarantulas was emerging to meet the visitor. The creature immediately jumped toward it.

"Oh!" Brooke yelped involuntarily.

It grabbed its prey with its front legs and shot its head forward to take a vicious bite out of the hapless tarantula. The creature devoured most of the spider in the space of fifteen seconds.

"Holy crap," said Chance. "Can you imagine if we hadn't gotten him in the case?"

Brandi shuddered at the thought of those teeth flying toward her face.

The creature found the other spiders in the case. It attacked and shredded them, just as it had done to the first.

Stuart's mouth hung open. "Oh my God..."

"That's some monster we've created," said Brooke.

Felix Strohm agreed. He stepped up to the terrarium to once again make sure the latch was secure.

CHAPTER 9

Chance stood on the balcony, releasing a long plume of smoke from his cigarette. His eyes followed the cloud as it rose in the humid air and veined off before dissipating. He took another long draw.

"I'm still freaked out by what just happened," said Brooke, standing next to Chance. She hadn't smoked in years, but today she was tempted to ask him for one.

"Yeah," Chance muttered. "That was something wild to go through." He turned his head and glanced at her, and he could see that she was still shaken. He wrapped his arm around her shoulders and drew her tighter. "Thank God for cages, huh?"

She chuckled nervously. "Right? That was close…Boris almost got loose."

He smiled. "We're officially calling it Boris," he noted. "What a terrible name."

Brooke shrugged.

The sliding glass door opened, and Stuart popped his head outside. "Hey, guys, dinner time."

Chance and Brooke went inside and sat down at the table. The rest of the group filled the other chairs, continuing their conversations about the birth of Boris. They were still animated.

"Can you believe how quickly Boris mastered control of his body?" Brandi marveled.

"It's terrifying," said Stuart. "He shouldn't have adjusted that quickly. I mean, the tissue from the surgery was barely repaired."

Chance tilted his head. "Maybe something to do with the proteins of my serum? Your guesses are as good as mine, at this point."

"Regardless," said Strohm, "it's a tremendous success. This is the dawn of a new era in regenerative medicine. Cheers to you all."

The others raised their glasses to his. "Cheers."

They finished their dinner, continuing their discussion of Boris. Then they thanked Oscar for yet another satisfying meal, got up, and went downstairs to check on their creation.

When they arrived at the laboratory, Strohm took a proud breath. Then he opened the door and the group of scientists entered. It only took a second for them to realize something was wrong.

The steel mesh covering the terrarium appeared to have been eaten through. A large, jagged hole was flayed outward.

Boris was gone.

"Um…" Brandi began.

"Ohshitohshit," said Stuart. His eyes dashed around the lab nervously.

Brooke was concerned. "How are we gonna find—"

Just then, something launched itself through the air toward Brooke. She squealed and ducked when she saw the blur of legs and teeth speeding at her.

The creature flew past and landed on the tile floor. Then it scampered away, dashing out of sight.

"No!" said Strohm. "He can't get away!"

Brooke's heart was racing. "Oh yes he can!"

"Come on," the billionaire urged. "We have to catch him!"

Brandi shook her head. "Oh hell no."

"We *have* to," said Strohm.

"He's right," said Chance. "If that animal gets out, it could screw up the ecosystem."

The group took a moment to think about it, and they agreed. They gathered their focus on what needed to be done.

The facility had to go into lockdown. They had to prevent the animal from getting out of the building. Strohm pressed the intercom button on the wall and announced to all personnel that a test animal had escaped. Then he instructed everyone to shut all doors and windows in the building.

"All right," Strohm said, "let's seal the place up room by room."

A bloodcurdling scream was heard on the main floor above them.

Brandi couldn't help but blurt, "Oh!"

"Let's go!" said Strohm.

"Hang on," said Stuart. "We need something to protect ourselves."

"You're right," Chance noted. "What can we use as a weapon?"

"Don't kill him," Strohm instructed. "He's too valuable."

"I'm not gonna try to kill him," said Chance, "but I *do* want to keep him from trying to kill *me*."

The others nodded emphatically.

"Okay, okay." Strohm looked around. "Well, let's see…those burlap sacks in the corner, grab those. And the trays over there. Maybe for, like, shields. And those surgical tools—but only as a last resort."

The group took up the sacks and makeshift weapons. Then, knowing the creature was elsewhere, they exited the laboratory and sealed it off.

The group crept up the stairs to the main floor. When they emerged from the stairwell, they saw nothing in the living area.

"Hello!" Strohm called out. "Oscar! Are you okay?"

There was no response from the housekeeper.

That was what Strohm was afraid of. The scream they'd heard sounded like Oscar's, and it was one of mortal peril.

"Oscar!" he repeated. Then, glancing at the others, he said, "C'mon, let's check the kitchen."

They worked their way to the kitchen, all the time scanning the corners of the room to make sure nothing could catch them by surprise.

Once they arrived at the kitchen, they saw pots and pans scattered all over the floor. Seconds later, they could see Oscar lying on the ceramic floor in the corner. Brandi screamed at the sight.

The cook's face was gone. Only some dark, wet remnants of meat remained, attached to his red skull. His throat had been devoured as well. A massive pool of blood surrounded the corpse.

Something clanked behind them.

Brooke yelped and jumped. Everybody whirled, but nothing was there. The group gripped their weapons tightly and held them as best they could in shaking hands.

"Oh God," Brandi whimpered. "Get me out of here! I can't do this!"

Brooke looked her directly in the eyes, trying to deliver strength. "Yes you can. Come on. We don't have a choice."

"It's imperative that we catch him," Hans reminded.

Brandi closed her eyes and took a deep breath. "Okayokayokay…what next?"

"Continue the search," Strohm said somberly. "Let's finish up downstairs, and then work our way all the way up."

The crew went back down the stairs and peered down the bottom-floor hallway. The door to the second lab, where the piranha specimens were kept, was partially open. That would be the next place to search.

They pulled the door all the way open and went inside to scan the room.

"There!" whispered Chance. "On the tank!"

Sure enough, the creature was crawling on the edge of the piranha tank. It walked the perimeter slowly, methodically, maintaining its balance.

"Out! Out!" Strohm said quietly. He ushered everybody out of the lab and quickly shut the door. "He's contained...thank God," he whispered, his remark accompanied by a sigh of relief. "We must keep him sealed in there."

The group peered through the glass portal on the door. They watched as the creature suddenly jumped into the water. Its legs clutched and secured one of the piranhas.

But it didn't kill. It just grabbed onto it tightly, convulsed rapidly, and then moved on to the next fish. Then the next, and the next.

"My God," said Stuart. "What's he doing?"

Brooke had a creepy feeling. "I think he's trying to impregnate the piranhas."

CHAPTER 10

The riverside bar was comforting. The juke box in the corner played some reggae, some favela funk, and some Brazilian rock—none of it too loud. The volume was perfect for enjoying the music while still being able to hold calm conversations. The air was marbled with smoke from cigars and cigarettes. And the Antarctica beers were ice cold.

Danny Kim and his first mate sat at the polished bar, relaxing with beer and hors d'oeuvres. After a good week of transporting goods and passengers, they would celebrate by spending the weekend in Manaus and having some fun.

"We had another good haul this week," said the captain, raising his bottle.

Guaré saluted back. "Business is good. We will have enough to update the boat in no time."

"Yes."

"And the bonus situation?"

Danny smiled. "I knew you would bring that up."

"Of course," said Guaré. "Incentive is exactly what it says it is."

The river captain reached into his pocket. "I did make that deal with you, and we did make that quota." He pulled out a stack of folded bills and started counting out his first mate's bonus pay.

"Thank you, Captain," Guaré grinned while receiving his money. "Now the big question is: what are we going to do over the weekend?"

Danny gazed upward into nothingness. "I am going to get drunk, sleep in a nice bed, and have a long, hot shower. And eat at our favorite restaurants."

"And after?"

"I think downriver. It's time to see my *balseira*."

Guaré nodded with a grin. His captain, like so many of the others, had river women that they frequented. It was a simple relationship: sex in exchange for diesel oil, money, or other gifts. Guaré, on the other hand, preferred to get his sex from women in the bars who were just looking for the same.

Danny caught sight of a new patron entering the bar. It was a white man, well groomed, dressed in a blue short-sleeve Au Noir shirt.

"Who's this now?"

Guaré turned to look. The man was walking toward the bar. He looked rich. "Tourist, I suppose."

"I suppose," the captain echoed.

The man took a stool next to Danny. He flagged the bartender down and ordered a beer. Then he turned to address the pair.

"Hello," he said to them.

"Hello," nodded Guaré.

"Listen, I'm looking for someone," the man announced. He pulled a photo up on his phone. "Her name is Monique Washington. She's been missing for almost two months now. I've been searching for her for six weeks."

The men looked at the picture and shook their heads. "Haven't seen her," said Danny.

"The last contact I had with her was from here, in Manacapuru. She had just bought a boat from one of the locals."

"Haven't seen her, *gae*," the captain repeated.

"Was she traveling with anyone else?" Guaré asked the man.

He shook his head. "She came alone."

"That's unusual," said Guaré.

The man did not reply, other than to say, "Well, thanks anyway."

Danny and Guaré watched him take his beer and move on. He stopped at the nearest table and asked the old man seated there the same question. They could hear the conversation, which became interesting.

"*Sim*, I know this woman," the patron said after seeing the photo.

"You do?" The searcher's voice was excited.

"I sold a boat to her," the old man said. "She paid me very well for it. I remember that."

"Do you have any idea where she might be now?"

"No. She said nothing about where she was taking it. Only that she was leaving at night. And that our transaction was to be kept quiet." He immediately realized he had just broken that vow. A guilty smile crawled up his cheeks.

"Is there any way of tracking the boat? Any kind of locater on board?"

The local shook his head. "No, sir."

"Would you have a picture of the boat?"

"No. Sorry."

The searcher sighed. "Okay. Well, thank you." He turned and walked away, heading to the next table.

"Another American," Guaré said when the man was out of earshot.

"Yes."

"First the billionaire, then the group of researchers, and now we hear of a missing American woman."

"Why would a woman be travelling the river at night alone?" Danny wondered.

"I don't know."

"Maybe she is a private investigator."

Guaré raised a finger. "Or a corporate spy."

"What do you mean?"

"Maybe she works for a competitor of Felix Strohm," said Guaré. "Maybe that man does, too."

"Could be."

"I wonder what Mr. Strohm is doing out there."

Danny had no idea, and he didn't really care.

"Why has he chosen to hide in the Amazon jungle?"

"Whatever Mr. Strohm is up to," Danny said, "he's trying to hide it from the rest of the world."

"And a woman may have gone missing because she tried to find it."

"Possible."

"I have a bad feeling. Something strange is going on up there," Guaré insisted.

"Of course," said Danny. "But we'll never know what it is."

"What if it's something bad? And we were the last ones to bring people there?"

Danny grimaced, then shrugged, and took another swill of his beer.

CHAPTER 11

Nobody had slept well that night. Their minds were still reeling from yesterday's wild events. One by one, the researchers came down from their bedrooms and shuffled to the dining table.

"Good morning, everyone," said Strohm when they were assembled. "Who wants coffee?"

Every person around the table gestured in the affirmative.

"Okay." The host retreated into the kitchen to grab the carafe and cups. He had brewed the coffee an hour ago, knowing Oscar was no longer there to do it. Strohm and the others would have to fend for themselves for meals now. At least until Strohm could hire another housekeeper.

Strohm had been up for most of the night. After collecting Oscar's body in a thick blanket, he and Hans had carried the corpse outside. They'd tossed their colleague into the Amazon River under dark of night. It seemed okay to let the wildlife feed on his remains—the circle of life.

Cleaning up the blood wasn't as bad as he'd figured. It only took him and Hans twenty minutes to sop up the blood, wipe the tiles, and disinfect the area. The towels were already halfway through the wash cycle in the laundry room.

Strohm poured the coffee. He could tell by the bags under his researchers' eyes that they had not slept much.

"I figure we could wing it for breakfast," the billionaire said. "We can all lend a hand cooking, or take turns, or just each cook for themselves. It's entirely up to the group."

"Do we have more raisin toast?" asked Stuart, whose stomach was growling.

Strohm nodded. "Yep. And eggs in the refrigerator, and milk, juice, and rice."

The group put together a makeshift breakfast. It was light, but it was enough to quell their hunger pangs. While they ate, they avoided the subject of Oscar's death. Since the body was gone and the kitchen was clean, everybody silently accepted the fact that the body had been given a proper burial. The group was content not speaking of it.

"So," said Strohm when they were finished eating. "I say we take a look at the lab and see what Boris is up to this morning."

It was inevitable. Everyone knew they would have to address the animal locked in the lab. But they were just as curious as their employer.

They put their dishes in the sink for later, and then they went to the video monitors next to the living area. Strohm activated one of the six monitors. It woke, brightening as it revealed its view of the lab.

"What the hell—" said Chance.

The video feed showed movement in the lab. A lot of movement.

"Oh my God," said Strohm. "Oh…my…"

The others looked at the monitor and were shocked by what they saw.

Not only had impregnation occurred, but dozens of baby creatures had already hatched. And they were already half the size of their parent. They scuttled all around the lab, wandering the floor and tables.

"What the hell?" Chance blurted. "That's not possible!"

Brooke stared in silent awe.

"It's not physically possible!" Chance continued. "Like, not at *all!*"

"Um…" said Stuart, "you're seeing it right before your eyes, just like we are."

"The serum," Brooke muttered.

Chance turned to her. "What?"

"The serum. Your serum had already allowed the genetic codes to accept each other. Maybe it also allowed Boris to share that genetic interpreter during physical mating."

Brandi's hands slid down her face. "Do you realize what you're saying? These creatures could just mate with any other animal and make new mutations!"

"No, I don't think so," said Brooke. "I think the cohesion is still limited to the two original sets of DNA."

"But still," Strohm stated, "this is alarming."

"My serum obviously sped up the reproductive process," said Chance. "This is crazy seeing these things the day after they were conceived."

"Terrifying," said Strohm.

Hans wasn't going to lie. "Fascinating. Absolutely fascinating. We've done something miraculous."

Strohm raised an eyebrow. "That's true. This might open up a whole new set of doors for medical breakthroughs."

Brandi tensed. For her, the sight was less of an inspiration. It was more of a nightmare. "I wish our phones worked," she said longingly. "What if we need to call someone?"

Strohm grinned. "We talked about this your first week here, remember? We may not have cellular signal out here, but I have the satellite phone. If there's an emergency, we'll use that."

"Where is the satellite phone?" asked Stuart.

"Oh, I—um—" Strohm paused. "I think I left it in the lab."

"Is that it there?" said Chance, pointing to a spot on the monitor screen.

The group spotted the satellite phone on an examination table amidst dozens of energetic creatures.

"We need to go get it," Manuel declared.

Strohm nodded. "Yes. We'll need that. All right, we're going in there."

"Don't forget," said Brandi, "Boris is still in there somewhere."

"I might need that specimen box," Strohm said. "Just in case we can get one or two of them inside for studying."

The billionaire went to the storage room and grabbed the steel specimen carrier, which was a solid box with a few tiny air holes. He also took a Maglite high-lumen flashlight. Then, he turned to the rest of the group and brought them to the stairway.

They moved down the steps to the bottom floor. Strohm led them down the hall to the laboratory doors. He peeked through the glass portal of the door.

He could swear the young animals looked bigger than they did five minutes ago. They were about eight inches long. The mass of hatchlings were crawling to and fro, but none of them were by the door at the moment.

Carefully, Strohm opened the door. He moved tentatively into the lab, and Manuel followed. Their presence was quickly noticed, and the creatures rushed toward them. Their eager jaws bit the air repeatedly, and the chattering of their teeth could be heard. Strohm turned the Maglite on. The intense beam of LED light hurt their eyes, making them retreat.

Manuel stepped closer to the table. When he got a good look at the satellite phone, he sighed. "The phone is destroyed."

Strohm was stunned. "Destroyed?" He joined his colleague at the table to see that the phone had been shredded, assuredly by strong teeth.

"Yeah," said Manuel. "Now we have no way of calling anybody."

Boris suddenly plopped down from atop a wall cabinet. The creature landed on the floor with a light *thump*, reset its legs, and sprang toward the men.

Strohm reacted. In one fluid motion, he dropped the flashlight and raised the metal box in front of him. Luckily, his aim was good and the attacking animal landed inside the box. Strohm instantly shut the cover and latched it. He could feel the spastic writhing from within as the animal sought to free itself.

The flashlight now harmlessly on the floor, the young creatures once again charged the human prey. Before Manuel could see them coming, they swarmed him. Crawling, biting, climbing. He screamed, stumbling backward, and tripped over a stool. They covered him when he hit the floor. Manuel frantically tried to get them off of him. The animals took chunks out of his hands when he brushed them. They bit with the ferocity of a buzz saw.

"Jesus!" Strohm picked up the Maglite, stepping back. He turned the LED beam on the swarm, but it did no good. Their brains were now completely committed to attacking their prey, ignoring the irritating light.

Manuel was bleeding badly from all over his body. The bites were everywhere, his clothing shredded and tissue devoured. His adrenaline allowed him to keep trying to fling the animals off, but each time he touched one, several sets of jaws rapidly took more of his hands. Manuel quickly lost enough blood that his body was too weak to move.

Strohm backed away to the door. There was nothing he could do for Manuel. He exited the lab and secured the door behind him.

"Ohmygod! Ohmygod!" cried Brooke. Her face was pale from the sight of the attack.

Chance held her, and she nuzzled into his chest and sobbed. Chance looked at Strohm. "What do we do now?"

"I—I don't know." Strohm and the others watched through the glass as the frenzied creatures spread out across the lab. They explored and tested barriers, failed to breach them, and moved on to the next ones. They were looking for a way out.

One of them tried the air vent on the wall. Its teeth were able to penetrate and rend the aluminum cover. Seeing this, the other animals joined. They started eating their way through the vent cover.

"We have to seal the vents!" said Brooke.

"How?"

"Any way we can! We can't let them get out!"

CHAPTER 12

The air vents connected every room of the facility. Once the creatures worked their way in, they would be able to hunt freely throughout the building. The only thing Felix Strohm could think of was to evacuate the facility and somehow kill everything left inside.

Fire was their only option.

"Listen, everyone!" Strohm said. "We don't have much time. We're gonna have to vacate the building and burn it from the inside out."

"What?" Brandi was already panicked, and the thought of destroying their current home made her heart pound even harder.

"I need you to quickly—and I mean *quickly*—gather what research records you can from the other lab, and then we're gonna kill the hatchlings."

"You've got to be kidding," said Brooke. "We'll be left vulnerable in the middle of the jungle!"

"Better than being trapped in here with those vicious things," Chance admitted. "I say let's do it."

"Now go, we only have minutes," said Strohm. He looked at Chance. "Most importantly, bring your serum."

"Okay."

"The research materials only, people!" stressed Strohm. "I can replace all your clothes and personal belongings. Just take what you're wearing and our work." He turned to Hans. "Come with me."

Strohm opened the heavy door and stepped outside. He ran through the foliage to the river, and Hans followed. They each grabbed a drum of diesel fuel from the pier. Then they dragged the drums back to the building and inside.

"All right," said Strohm, "do we have everything we can take?" Seeing filled arms and nodding heads, he said, "Upstairs, everyone!"

The others hurried up the stairway. Their nerves were peaked with stress and anxiety. They had no idea how much time they had before the creatures were swarming the entire facility.

Strohm and Hans poured out most of the fuel, covering the lower floor in the pungent liquid. Then they hauled what was left up the steps to join their companions on the main floor. Strohm emptied the drums on the staircase and the majority of the main floor.

"I need a lighter," said Strohm.

Chance pulled his cigarette lighter from his pocket and handed it over.

"Give me the serum," Strohm directed. Chance handed the vials to him, and Strohm stuffed them in his pocket. "Okay, now go to the front door there and get outside. As soon as I light this, I'm running out and shutting the place up."

Hans took the carrier holding Boris to free his employer's hands. He and the others opened the door and rushed outside.

Strohm moved to the edge of the pooled diesel. Making sure the front door was open and his escape path was ready, he picked up a napkin. He ignited it with the lighter. As the flames began their dance up the paper, Strohm tossed it into the fuel and ran for the door.

The diesel went up fiercely with a *whoosh*. The fire raced across the floor and down the stairway. Another *whoosh* could be heard when the lower level caught fire.

Strohm shut the steel door and joined the group.

"Holy crap," said Stuart, "I can hear it from out here."

"Yes." Strohm ushered the others with his hands. "Come on, let's get some distance from it. Who knows what might explode in there when the fire hits it."

Brandi nodded fervently. "Definitely."

They hurried to the edge of the river. Once they were on the pier, they turned to look at the facility.

There were muffled explosions from within. Strohm felt his pocket to make sure he still had the serum in his possession. Relieved that he did, he stood next to Boris's box and watched his facility be destroyed by the inferno.

The flames were now visible through the windows. Brooke feared that the intense heat would cause thermal stress and break the glass. That was inevitable with a burning building; it was just a matter of time. When the windows did crack and shatter, she prayed she wouldn't see any hybrid creatures escape through the broken windows.

The same fear took hold of the others. They looked anxiously. But to their relief, the only thing pouring out of the building was black smoke.

Whatever monstrous creatures were inside were dead now. Suffocated, and then burnt to a crisp. The group had solved the terrible problem they had created. But now, they were in a new predicament.

"What do we do now?" worried Brandi. "We're alone in the middle of the jungle!"

Felix Strohm, for once, was at a loss for words.

"We should follow the river," said Hans. "It will eventually lead to people."

Chance nodded. "Yes. Good idea."

"That could take days!" said Brandi. "Maybe weeks! Do you know how many things in the jungle could kill us in that time?"

"I do," Brooke said matter-of-factly. She was well aware of the jaguars, black caimans, dart frogs, wandering spiders, pit vipers, and green anacondas that were native to the area. "That's why we'll stay together. No straying apart."

Stuart agreed. "That's what we've gotta do, then." He tried to keep his voice calm, but he was terrified that the jungle was going to take them.

"Look!" Chance blurted out.

Everyone looked up and saw what he had spotted.

A boat was gliding into the tributary, heading their way. They recognized it straight away. It was the same forty-foot river boat that had brought them to this remote location. And in the wheelhouse was the familiar face of Danny Kim.

"Hey!" they all yelled, waving frantically.

Guaré's head popped into view, and he waved back.

"Oh thank God," sighed Brandi. "Thank God."

The boat veered toward shore to pick up the grateful passengers.

CHAPTER 13

"I still can't believe you showed up and saved us."

Danny reacted indifferently. "Just lucky, I guess." He kept his eyes on the river ahead.

Strohm was still confused. "What were you doing this far into the jungle?"

Guaré glanced at his captain, and then at the group of passengers. "We just had a strange feeling that you might need help, so we came up to check on you."

The billionaire patted Guaré's shoulder. "Well, thank you. Thank you both."

"Yeah," said Chance. "You probably saved our lives."

The captain looked back to acknowledge Chance. He grinned and smacked his chest.

Chance returned the primitive gesture, adding a smile that was friendly and grateful.

The steel box rattled. The noise brought everybody's attention to it.

"What's in the box?" Guaré asked.

Stuart laughed out loud, uncontrollably. This prompted the rest of the researchers to laugh as well.

The first mate was confused. "What?"

Strohm's finger swayed side to side. "Oh no, my friend, you don't want to see what's in there."

"Now I surely do."

"This is an animal that we've been working on," said Strohm. "You know, like surgery to make it stronger in the wild."

The researchers cringed at the thought of creatures like Boris being free in the jungle. God only knew what the ecological consequences would be.

"What kind of animal?" Guaré asked.

"I'm sorry. It's a classified project."

The first mate conceded that he was not to know about the secret. He nodded and changed the subject. "I am sorry to hear about the accident at your lab. We saw the smoke."

"We don't know exactly how the fire started," said Strohm, embellishing the story, "but it was uncontrollable. It's a miracle we got out when we did."

Nobody from the group spoke to the contrary.

Their journey back to civilization had begun. Miles of lush green shoreline went by. Eventually the group saw other boats traveling the river, which reassured them; they were going to rejoin the rest of society. They were immensely thankful for everything working out the way it did that day.

As the hours passed, more and more river traffic was visible. By the time the boat reached Manacapuru, it was early in the evening. The sun was low in the sky behind them as Danny docked his boat.

"Thank you," Strohm said to the captain, shaking his hand. "I'll make sure you are rewarded for getting us safely here."

Danny Kim gave a curt nod. "Aye."

The passengers exited the boat and said goodbye to the captain and first mate. The next thing to do was get a ride. Now that their cellular phones had signal, Strohm called for a car. Then he brought the group to a bar to wait while they cooled down, got something to eat, and hydrated themselves.

A black Lincoln Navigator arrived a while later. Seeing it through one of the windows, Strohm led the group outside to meet it. A familiar face stepped out and greeted his fare.

"Greetings, Mr. Strohm. Everyone."

"Hello, Benny," said Strohm. "I'm glad you were able to pick us up. We need to get to Manaus. And then we'll be going to the airport tomorrow."

"Yes sir." The driver opened the Navigator's doors and got his guests seated. "No bags?" he asked, surprised.

"No, I'm afraid not," Strohm said. "Just us and everything we're holding."

"Yes sir."

The creature in the box had settled down. Strohm shook it, just a little, and felt the animal move inside. Boris was still alive.

An hour and a half later, the vehicle was in the city of Manaus. Benny delivered the group to a prominent hotel. Strohm led the group to the desk to check in. He got three rooms for everyone, and they brought their research to Strohm's room.

It was after sundown. The group was starving. What they needed was a large, satisfying meal to nourish their bodies and soothe their souls. After the late dinner, they returned to the hotel and to their beds.

Their heads were flooded with thoughts. They reflected on their research, their many weeks of experimental surgery, and the tragic deaths of Oscar and Manuel. Sheer exhaustion won out, however, and sleep soon took them.

*   *   *

The following morning, Benny returned to the hotel to take the group to the airport. He helped them load their things and drove them off.

"I called Manuel's family late last night," Strohm informed his team. "It was hard, but I had to notify them of his passing."

"I was wondering about that," said Stuart. "I mean, like, would they need his body for a death certificate?"

"I told them he fell out of a boat and his body was never recovered."

"And Oscar?" said Chance.

Strohm shrugged. "To my knowledge, he had no family."

The SUV took them through the streets of Manaus. The passengers took in the sights of the city for the last time. A multitude of busses, cyclists, stained concrete walls, hospitals, supermarkets, and majestic buildings went by. The group passed by the historic Amazon Theater, an immense opera house with a glorious, colorful tiled dome on its roof. They saw a variety of churches, some antiquated and some ultra-modern.

Benny pulled into Strohm's private hangar at the airfield. There, the group spilled out of the vehicle. They noticed the same Gulfstream jet that had brought them to Brazil two months ago. The pilot was already leaving the cockpit to come down the steps and greet the travelers.

The sight of the plane brought comfort to Stuart. "I can't wait to get home," he sighed.

"Neither can I," said Strohm.

"I'm sorry you lost the labs," said Brooke. "It's a shame. What a waste."

"Don't fret," the billionaire grinned. "We may have lost one facility, but at least we accomplished our goal. And we have Boris here to show for it."

"What now?" asked Chance.

"Back to the States," said Strohm. "Back to my property, where I have another laboratory. There we can pick up where we left off here."

CHAPTER 14

The plane climbed quickly in the sky.

Looking out the window, Brandi watched the trees of the jungle shrink and blend together as they fell farther below. The treetops looked like an endless sea of bunched broccoli.

"It looks nice from up here," she remarked.

Brooke peered out her window. "Yeah, it does. But it was nice down there too."

Brandi flashed her a look. "Seriously?"

"Well, yes."

"Um, let me remind you that we almost *died* down there. Not to mention poor Oscar and Manuel."

"I know," said Brooke, "but the jungle itself was beautiful. The trees, the smells...especially the sounds of all the wildlife around us. We were immersed in nature. And we got to live right on the

Amazon River! Not many people in the world get a chance to do that."

"I suppose," Brandi said. "But all the same, I can't wait to get home."

"You're not *actually* going home, are you?" asked Stuart, seated behind her. He seemed concerned.

Brandi wanted to, but she had signed on to be a part of this research team. She pivoted her swiveling chair to better see Stuart before replying.

Strohm interjected. "In light of everything that has happened, I want you all to know that if any of you wish to quit the project, I would understand. You would still get paid for the time you've put in."

The group was silent.

"But remember," Strohm cautioned, "you'll still be held to your non-disclosure agreement. Not just for the duration of your employment, but forever. You each know that from the contracts you signed."

They nodded.

"So decide. When we land in California, the plan is to bring you to my home in Newport Beach. There are more than enough guest rooms for you there, and the laboratory is on the property. Otherwise, if you choose to be out, I'll arrange to have you flown to wherever you wish to go."

Chance looked up. "I plan on staying on," he declared, glancing at Brooke. He truly hoped she would be with him.

She met his gaze. "So do I," she said.

"I'm not quitting," said Stuart.

Brandi hesitated. This was her chance to get out of the nightmare, to be home, to begin the rest of her life. But the scientist inside her couldn't do that. They were in the process of making history. "I'm still in."

"Excellent," Strohm said with a smile that expressed his delight and thankfulness. "A group of true professionals."

He then turned his attention to their creation in the steel box. Strohm picked the box up and set it on his lap. The creature shifted inside, and Strohm felt the movement through the metal.

"He's still alive, thank God," said Strohm. "This specimen, plus your serum and the research material, will greatly aid us in progressing our experiments."

"The animal must be thirsty," said Chance. "And hungry."

"I'm sure," nodded Strohm. "Although I gave him some water this morning before we left the hotel."

Stuart was curious. "How?"

"Easy, actually. I just poured some through the little holes and let it collect on the bottom. He seemed to enjoy it."

"What can we feed it?" said Brandi.

Strohm thought hard. "Well, I need to find something that I can squeeze inside through the holes. Something small, but with protein." He got up and went to the airplane's aft galley.

He opened the storage pantry and perused the shelves. There was a jar of peanuts; those could possibly fit. Then he checked the refrigerator. Seeing packs of string cheese, he grabbed those as well.

He brought the food to his chair and sat down. Starting with the peanuts, he opened the jar and tried to push a nut through one of the air holes. It was a little too big. Strohm separated the peanut in half and tried again. Each half went through, and he dropped them inside. Then he pressed half a dozen more in.

The creature took a moment to figure out what it was given. Once it determined the objects were food, it greedily devoured them.

Strohm grinned. "He likes it."

Next, he peeled strands of string cheese and fed them into the box. Feeling the activity inside the box, Strohm was pleased that Boris was being fed.

"Don't worry, my friend," Strohm said softly. "We'll have you in your new home before the end of the day."

CHAPTER 15

The jet landed at John Wayne Airport in Santa Ana, California. The pilot touched down smoothly and braked to slow them. Then he taxied the plane to their destination hangar.

The door opened, and the passengers descended the stairs. They were relieved that their flight was over. There was a comfort in being back in the States. Instead of being buried deep in the jungle, surrounded by danger and isolation, they were back in their familiar, convenient, comfortable society.

A stretched Cadillac XTS was parked outside the hangar. The chauffeur stood next to the black limousine, waiting for his employer. "Good afternoon, sir," he said earnestly. "How were your travels?"

Strohm approached with his team. "Pretty good, Stephen. We've had some success, and now we're all going to conclude the research at the lab here."

"Very good, sir." The chauffeur corralled everybody inside the car. Then he planted himself in the driver seat and pulled the Cadillac away from the private hangar.

Half an hour later, the car arrived at Felix Strohm's estate. The billionaire had a gated sixty-acre property on the Pacific shore. The limo entered through the security gate and headed down the driveway, which was decorated with rows of colorful flowers and finely-trimmed shrubs. Two structures were seen ahead. The smaller one, assuredly, was the laboratory. The larger was an immense house.

It was a bright limestone Italian-Renaissance-style home with distinctive red Mediterranean tile roofing. The ten-thousand-square-foot mansion was remarkable.

"Wow," Chance muttered. "Look at that."

Brooke was impressed. "I figured he would have more of a post-modern house. But this, this is classy."

Strohm, overhearing the chatter, turned in the front passenger seat to look back. "Thank you. But just wait until you see the inside."

Stephen parked in front of the house. Everyone trickled out of the vehicle and gathered at the entrance to the house. Strohm, still carrying the box containing Boris, was excited to be home.

The front door opened, revealing a tall man with slick black hair. He smiled amiably at the sight of their arrival. "Hello, Mr. Strohm. Welcome home."

Strohm introduced him. "Everybody, this is my chief of staff: Bradley."

They all nodded and said hello.

"Come in, sir," said Bradley. "I just got back from the lab. Everything is ready; the equipment is here, and the fish were brought today by Co—"

Strohm cut him off. "Thank you, Bradley. That's wonderful news." He addressed his guests. "Come on in, everyone." He entered his home, and the group followed.

The interior had high ceilings. A large crystal chandelier hung above in the entryway. It looked—naturally—very expensive. As they walked further to begin their tour of the new lodging, they were treated to the sights of Romanesque sculptures, crystal table ornaments, and a prideful number of abstract paintings.

"This is the living area," said Strohm, gesturing toward the grand room holding two ivory leather sectional sofas, a lavish entertainment center, and cubism-inspired tables. One of the side walls had a sliding glass door leading outside.

"That's the west patio. There's an infinity pool, if you want to swim. Or, you can just head to the private beach right below."

Brooke's eyes lit up when she heard that. "Oh my God, that would be so peaceful."

Strohm raised his head admirably to the sky. "You can see the most beautiful sunsets from there."

They moved on to see the kitchen, which had appliances unlike any the group had ever seen. There was a sixty-inch double-oven gas range, two integrated refrigerators, an ice maker, and two dishwashers.

"This is awesome," said Stuart. "I assume you have a chef?"

Strohm nodded. "Antoine, whom you'll meet this evening."

Brandi was anticipating a gourmet meal tonight. "Nice."

"How many staff are in the house?" asked Chance.

"Not as many as usual," said Strohm. "Mostly because I was out of the country. That, and my time and energies are currently devoted to one job. Ours.

"My live-in staff are always here," he continued. "You've already met my chief of staff. Bradley manages everyone, including the security team, Javier the groundskeeper, and Marta the housemaid. Plus, he also acts on my behalf with some of my corporate duties."

"That's extremely helpful," said Brooke.

Strohm smiled. "I pay him extremely well. Anyway, now that we're back here for the duration of the project, you'll see others who come here daily to work. Like my chauffeur Stephen, Marta the housemaid, and Antoine. Antoine's dishes are always a treat, by the way."

"I can't wait," said Stuart.

"In the meantime," Strohm said, "let's continue our tour."

The group followed their host up a stairway winding along the walls. They were shown the guest bedrooms on the second floor. Each was equipped with a king-size mattress, an antique armoire, soothing lighting and wall colors, and an en suite bathroom.

The rest of the house took half an hour to see. Strohm took them to the library, the home gym, the movie theater, and the four-lane bowling alley.

"Your home is lovely," said Brooke.

Strohm tried not to beam. "Thank you. But now, most importantly, I want to show you where we'll be working."

With Boris in hand, he led them outside and to the other building that was a hundred yards away from the house. They got to the main entrance's steel door. Strohm showed them the keypad that controlled the door.

"I'll bet you'll never guess what the code to this is," he said playfully.

"Let me guess," said Chance. "Two-four-six-eight?"

"Bingo." Strohm opened the door and escorted the group inside.

The lab was much bigger than the one in Brazil. A vast fifty-foot-by-fifty-foot room, it was set up similarly to the previous one. There was a long, narrow steel tank with water piping through it, a museum-sized terrarium, examination tables, microscopes, flasks, beakers, pipettes, analyzing equipment, surgical tools, and two operating tables.

"Déjà vu," said Brandi.

"I even had more specimens flown in," Strohm informed them. "They were delivered just this morning."

The group wandered to the long tank and peered down to see foot-long red-bellied piranhas, swimming around and acclimating to their new environment.

"Let's get this poor, tired fellow home," said Strohm. He walked to the terrarium and opened the top. He raised the steel box containing Boris, teetering it on the edge. Then, taking a deep breath, he unlocked the door to the box and shook it open.

The creature tumbled out, flailing its hairy legs. Its jaws clamped on the lid in an attempt to hang on. The bite was timed too late, and the animal's teeth didn't get a good enough grip to stop its body's momentum. It fell through the vegetation in the terrarium and landed on the sandy floor.

Strohm quickly closed the terrarium's top and latched it secure.

The others joined him there, watching to see how their creation would react. The creature was weary from the journey, however, and moved slowly. It found its water supply in the corner, where it went to drink and rehydrate.

"I'd better feed him," said Strohm. "Hang on, I'll be right back." He left the lab.

Brooke watched the creature drink. "I'm still amazed by what we've done," she muttered.

"We're not done," Chance said. "I can't imagine what our next step will be."

"I'm sure it'll have something to do with your serum," said Brandi. "That formula will be instrumental in our advancement of regenerative therapy."

Strohm returned with a thick slice of ham in his hand. He approached the case slowly.

"Okay, everyone," he said, "stand back."

He unlatched the top and held the handle firmly. After a second of focus, he opened the top enough to drop the ham into the tank. He let loose of the meat, shut the top, and locked it shut again.

The hungry animal flipped around and went for the ham. It took a bite, chewed, and then continued taking rapid, greedy bites of the meat.

"Let's leave him be for the night," said Strohm. "For now, let's go back to the house and get ready for dinner ourselves."

The group vacated the lab. They were more than happy to enjoy a hearty meal. Afterward, which they were probably even happier about, they would sleep deeply.

CHAPTER 16

The group had slept for almost ten hours. One by one they woke and came downstairs to the living area. They were each wearing the pajamas and robes Strohm provided in the guest rooms. Once they were seated at the dining table, they were served coffee or tea, and given a nourishing breakfast.

"After you eat," said Strohm, "what say we get out for a day of shopping? You all need new clothes and stuff, especially since I made you leave everything in the lab we had to abandon."

"I was going to address that myself," said Brooke. "'Cause yeah, we've been wearing the same clothes for the past two days."

"I know, I know. As was I! But now that we're back in civilization, you'll need new everything. I'll call for the limo and Stephen will take you all out for the day. Get new clothing, toiletries, razors, whatever you need. Stephen will have one of my credit cards to take care of it all."

"Thank you, Mr. Strohm," said Stuart. "We'd all appreciate that very much."

"My pleasure," the billionaire smiled, folding his hands. "It's the least I could do."

Brandi was thrilled. "This is gonna be great! Um, but what are we going to wear to go out?"

"Your clothes from last night have been laundered," Strohm announced. "Marta should be bringing them back to your rooms right about now."

When breakfast was over, the researchers went to their rooms to get ready for the day. As told, their clothes were clean and folded on their beds. Those who had not yet showered did so. Thirty minutes later, they had all gathered at the entryway.

The chauffeur was waiting in the driveway. He loaded them up, nodded to his employer, and drove them off for a day of shopping.

Strohm stayed behind. Not only was it unnecessary for him to go along, but he had business here to attend to.

He walked to the adjacent laboratory building. Punching the code in, he entered and turned the lights on.

Boris had adapted to his new surroundings. The creature had made a corner nest in the sand. It seemed complacent in the makeshift terrarium. When it saw Strohm approach, however, it grew agitated.

Strohm brought his face to the glass to study their specimen. The animal sprang toward his face, smacking into the glass. Strohm jerked away instinctively.

"You're quick," he said to the creature. "Pascavage will like that."

The animal stood tensed, its legs flexed and trembling. It was clearly wanting to kill and devour the prey in its sight.

Strohm pulled out his phone and dialed the number for his contact representing the party that had contracted him. After two rings, the call was picked up.

"Pascavage here," said a man with a thick voice.

"Hello, Colonel. Felix Strohm."

"Strohm," the man acknowledged. "I take it you're back home now."

"Yes sir, we arrived yesterday late afternoon."

"Your piranhas were delivered yesterday morning, just as you asked. And the arachnids will be there in two days."

"Yes, I saw the fish. Thank you for accommodating so promptly."

"Naturally," said the man. "Anything you need for the completion of this project."

"You're going to be pleased with the results so far," Strohm stated. "Once you see the subject animal, you'll be satisfied with our progress."

"Now that you've returned with the prototype, I want to see it up close."

"Yes, Colonel," said Strohm. "You may come by right now, if you wish."

"Outstanding," the colonel responded. "I'm on my way."

CHAPTER 17

A black Hummer was let through the security gate and onto Strohm's estate. It was driven by Colonel Brad Pascavage of the U.S. Army. The colonel sat high in the driver's seat, gripping the wheel commandingly. He was excited to see the creature his billionaire contractor had told him about.

Strohm was waiting on the front porch when Pascavage pulled up. He stepped over to the Hummer when it stopped. When the colonel stepped out, Strohm met him with a handshake.

"Good afternoon, Colonel," said Strohm.

"Felix," returned the colonel. A cordial grin graced the bald man's square jaw. "It's good to see you again. I can't wait to see the work you've done."

"Well then, let's not waste any time. Come, let's go to the lab."

Pascavage pulled his uniform tight and followed Strohm to the laboratory. They went inside, heading directly for the terrarium.

"Holy shit." The colonel could barely believe his eyes. He was mesmerized by the sight of such a hideous creature. It was nightmarish. As Pascavage approached the tank, the animal bristled and gnashed its teeth at him. It charged against the glass. The colonel didn't even flinch. "It's perfect."

Strohm was pleased by Pascavage's reaction. "He's an amazing animal. We've broken barriers to get to where we are now. He even reproduces."

"You're shitting me."

"No, sir, it's true. He got loose in my last lab, found his way to the other piranha specimens, and mated with them. He can reproduce with other members of his host species."

Pascavage leaned closer. "Incredible."

"And that is why I requested the shipment of piranhas to be delivered here."

The colonel nodded contentedly. "I see. That's the next step, then? To have them ready for production?"

"Yes, sir."

"I'd like to see some more enhancements first, before we get to that stage."

Strohm frowned. "Oh? Like what, exactly?"

"Well, it seems readily suitable for release in enemy jungles or forests. The Army would like it to also be able to take to the air."

"You're kidding me."

"I am not," Pascavage said. "Could we incorporate some wings somehow?"

"Colonel, even if we were able to do something like that, how would you control it? It will be difficult enough to contain the animal as it is once it's unleashed in enemy territory. Add the ability to take flight? That's too much to control."

"You just let the Army worry about that," said Pascavage. His voice was stern, letting the billionaire know who was in charge.

The gentlemen spent a couple of hours discussing their goals and timetables. After that, the colonel was content. He returned to his Hummer with Strohm in tow.

"We will meet the deadline," Strohm assured the colonel. "No doubt about it."

Pascavage let loose a tight grin. "Excellent." He got into his Hummer and started the engine. Before pulling away, he lowered the driver-side window and said, "Keep me posted regularly, just as you have been."

Strohm gave Colonel Pascavage a thumbs-up and watched his vehicle roll down the driveway.

*   *   *

The group had finished shopping and was coming back to the estate. It hadn't taken as long as they'd thought it would to acquire all the clothing and toiletries they needed. Stephen steered up the long driveway to the house.

A black Hummer was coming toward them. The occupants of the limo noticed, and they kept their eyes on it as it approached them.

The driver was a military man, as they could see stripes on his uniform. He met their gaze as he went by. Oddly, he presented them with a salute before he passed.

"Who was that?" asked Chance.

"I don't know, sir," said Stephen. "But I've seen him come and go before."

Brooke was curious. "Did he just salute us?"

"I think he did," said Chance. "That was strange, wasn't it?"

The limo stopped in front of the house, and Stephen stepped out to help with the bags. The group saw Strohm standing there.

"Who was that?" Brooke asked him.

"That's classified, I'm afraid," said Strohm.

"What?" Stu scoffed. "Come on."

"Yeah," said Chance, "he even saluted us on our way in."

Strohm said nothing. His face registered indecision.

Brandi acted on it. "Yeah, Mr. Strohm, he knows us but we don't know him. Does he have something to do with our project?"

"Well…" Strohm said, stalling.

"We need to know," said Brooke. The thought of military personnel tied into their scientific endeavors concerned her.

The billionaire sighed. "Okay. Yes, our project is funded by the Department of Defense. The Army, to be specific."

Chance had a sickening feeling in the pit of his stomach. "This is a military project…"

"Why didn't you tell us before?" Brandi said.

Strohm threw his hands up. "Look, I'm not even supposed to tell you now!" he lied. "Okay? This project is highly classified. Need-to-know, blah, blah. They're very serious about that. So, as far as you're concerned, I never said anything about it to you."

The group exchanged unsure looks with each other.

"This doesn't change anything," said Strohm. "The work we're doing is just as important regardless of who is paying for it."

Still doubt on their faces.

"Look at the big picture. Our advances will still lead to bigger things. Like replacing diseased tissue and organs with stronger ones. Maybe even curing cancer."

"I suppose," Stuart allowed.

"Now come on, get your things put away inside. We'll be having dinner at six."

*   *   *

After dinner, the two couples excused themselves from their employer and took a walk to the beach together. The sunset was a deep orange, almost red. It was beautiful, but the group's minds were too heavy with concern to appreciate it that evening.

"I told you," said Brooke. "Remember, in Brazil, when I was worried he was making something for the government?"

"I do," said Chance, lighting a cigarette.

"You suspected that?" Stuart asked. "What made you think that?"

Brooke shrugged slightly. "Look what we made: a superpredator. We didn't need to go as far as we did to test our theories. But Mr. Strohm just kept going with it. And now we have a vicious killing machine. And it can reproduce way too quickly for my comfort."

"What would the military want with that?" Brandi pondered.

"Maybe an animal they could use against an enemy camp, I dunno."

Stuart chuckled. "Jesus. Like bioweapons."

"Exactly," said Brooke. "Bioweapons that can hunt."

Chance was not convinced. "They can't be that stupid. What makes them think they could ever control these animals?"

"They could just drop 'em into enemy territory and let 'em loose," said Stuart. "Maybe they figure they could come in afterward and clean up the area."

"There's no way they could contain them all," Chance argued. "Even if they killed a bunch, some would surely disappear into the jungle or wherever and destroy the balance of that ecosystem."

Brooke smirked. "And since when has the military cared about their effect on places they wage war?"

The group silently agreed.

"So," said Brandi, "the big question is: what do we do now, knowing we're helping create a possible war weapon?"

Brooke looked out across the waves and into the darkening sky. "I don't know."

CHAPTER 18

Strohm thought long and hard the night before. He knew that after sleeping on it, some members of the team might decide to leave the project, especially when he would have to tell them what the next phase of the project entailed: wings on their predator.

He was going to have to meet them head-on, countering their objections with a convincing reason to stay on board. He couldn't afford to lose them now. Without them, there was no way Strohm would be able to deliver what the Army was asking for.

They met for breakfast, taking their seats at the dining table. The conversation was tepid. There was a discomfort in the room, despite everybody's token comments and remarks about the food. Each person there knew what was really on everyone's mind. The topic needed to be addressed.

"Listen, Mr. Strohm," Brandi began, "we've been doing a lot of thinking."

"I can imagine," said Strohm.

"I can't speak for everyone," she continued, "but I think I need to remove myself from this project."

Here we go, he thought.

Brooke nodded. "Me too."

Strohm needed to quell the dissension immediately. "My friends, please, listen."

The group stared at him, waiting for what he had to say.

"I am sorry," said Strohm. "I'm sorry for keeping information from you. Bear in mind, I was ordered to keep you in the dark about our endgame," he fibbed again. "But from this day on, I promise you all nothing but complete honesty and transparency.

"That being said," he continued, "here's what the Army wants from us next. They were so impressed with our work linking the circulatory and nervous systems of the piranha and the tarantula, that they want us to push the boundaries a little more."

Chance was curious. "How so?"

"They've instructed us to augment Boris by finding a way to incorporate winged ability."

"Um, what?" said Stuart, thinking he hadn't heard correctly.

Strohm smiled. "Wings."

"Oh, hell no," Brandi blurted.

Strohm held up one hand to request her patience.

"Despite what we are being asked to do by the Army, our personal goal is something else. From the very beginning, I was using their project and its funding to accomplish exactly what I'd told you on day one. My primary goal is to advance regenerative medicine, which we've been able to do under the radar during this project. So...," he shrugged, "no matter how ugly the means, we still have the opportunity to make medical history that can save lives. We can fulfill our obligation with the Army while achieving our own goal."

The words steeped in the group's brains. Was their employer being honest? And if so, could they live with the thought of creating monsters for the military in order to make history that would benefit countless lives in the future?

"Okay," Stuart finally said. "I think I can deal with that."

Chance had swung the same way. "I think I can too."

Brandi was on the fence about this. But after Brooke voiced her intent to stay, Brandi decided to remain with her colleagues.

"Excellent," said Strohm. He couldn't help but grin.

They bought it, he thought smugly.

After breakfast, Antoine cleared the table and disappeared into the kitchen. The group remained seated at the table, discussing the next phase of their experimentation. The first thing they would need to do was decide which variety of bird they would use. It would have to be a larger bird with wings strong enough to lift the body of their creature. Perhaps the wings of a gull, hawk, or small owl.

Next would come the impossible task. How could they physically add wings to the arachnid body? They considered removing the two middle pairs of legs and connecting the wings to that muscle tissue.

The group ventured outside and started walking to the laboratory. They wanted to check on Boris, make sure the animal was all right, and then they would begin their list of what they needed.

"Obviously," said Stuart, "we'll need several bird specimens brought in."

"That won't be a problem," Strohm said. "We have unlimited resources. We can get anything we ask for."

"It'll be trial and error, naturally," said Stuart, "figuring out how to incorporate wings with the spider's body."

"You'll need to make some more of that serum," Strohm said to Chance.

"I'll start on that right away," Chance affirmed.

Strohm unlocked the door and they entered the lab. When the lights were flicked on, the group was shocked by what they saw.

Boris had escaped.

The terrarium was on the floor, now just shattered glass, vegetation, and a mess of wet dirt and sand.

Brandi gasped, her heartbeat fluttering fearfully. Her skin tightened. "Where is he?" she whispered.

The group tensed while they began scanning the large room.

There was movement atop the piranha tank, and their eyes darted to it. They saw Boris lying on the corner of the edge, stretching his legs.

"Oh no," said Brooke, "I think he mated again."

"Dammit!" Strohm hissed. "All of those fish were for more experimenting. Now we're going to have another army of hatchlings."

"Not if we kill everything before they're born," said Brooke.

Chance agreed. "Yeah. We need to kill them all somehow."

The billionaire stiffened his back. "There is no way we're killing Boris! We've come too far with him to lose him as a subject."

Before the group could decide on a plan, the creature heard and spotted the humans. Its brain commanded it to attack.

It sprang from the tank and dashed toward the group.

Adrenaline shot through the researchers as they saw fierce teeth scuttling their way.

"Go! Go!" said Strohm. He and his team ran for the door. They bullied it open, rushed outside, and shut the steel door behind them.

They heard the *thud* of the animal striking the door.

"Jesus, lock it! Lock it!" Brandi cried.

"It's locked!" Strohm assured

Panting, the group leaned against the concrete building and tried to calm their pounding hearts.

"How did he get out, goddammit?" yelled Strohm. Frustration was making the veins in his neck and forehead swell.

"He must've toppled the tank somehow," Chance offered. "Maybe he—" He rammed his fist into his hand. "—*attacked* the glass until the tank started to sway, got some sort of momentum, and managed to fall over."

"I can't believe it," Stuart mumbled. His mind was reeling.

"Who cares how?" said Brandi. "All that matters is what do we do now?"

The group was silent for a moment. They could hear the repeated smacking on the door.

"Call the Army," Brooke suggested. "I'm sure they can send some personnel here to take care of it."

Strohm was hesitant. "We can't do that. If they get wind of this embarrassing situation, they'll probably pull the plug on our project and give it to someone else."

"I doubt that," said Chance.

"We have to take care of this ourselves," Strohm insisted. "Let's get back to the house and figure something out."

CHAPTER 19

Strohm was wrestling with his feelings. On one hand, the result of their work was invaluable, but on the other, they were facing another situation that had to be neutralized before it got out of their control. The group knew that the birth of new hatchlings was inevitable now. Multiple offspring running loose in the lab would overtake and kill the research team. Even worse, they could escape the laboratory and work their way into neighborhoods and attack the public.

"I just don't know," said Strohm. "I don't know what we should do."

"Really?" Brooke said in disbelief.

He held up a hand defensively. "I know we're gonna have to exterminate the offspring, but how? And is there any way to recapture Boris and keep him secure?"

"I don't think so," said Chance. "That thing finds a way to escape too often. I say we kill Boris along with the rest of them, and then we can start over, in a different direction."

"But this is the direction the Army requested," said Strohm.

"Well, then we can do it again, but only after we've found a sure-fire way to keep that kind of animal contained. Until then, we need to kill everything in that lab."

Strohm's eyes drooped toward the floor. "All of our hard work…"

"I agree with Chance," Stuart declared. "Kill all of them, including Boris."

"*Especially* Boris," Brandi muttered. There was no mistaking her pure fear.

Strohm looked at Hans, who reluctantly agreed with a nod.

"All right," said Strohm. "We'll kill everything in there."

"How about fire?" Brooke proposed. "That did the trick last time."

Strohm liked the suggestion. "That's probably the best option we have."

"Will the lab hold up to a fire inside?" Brandi wondered. "I mean, the structure itself. I don't want it to break apart and let them out."

"No worry there," said Strohm. "The walls are extra-thick concrete. It's impenetrable. Even earthquake proof."

"What do we use to create a sufficient fire?" Chance said.

Everybody brainstormed. All of the chemicals they could use were locked inside the lab. They were left with only everyday items as options.

"Do you have any containers of gasoline?" asked Brandi.

Strohm frowned. "Just a little, maybe, in the garage."

Brooke thought about other flammable gasses. "Propane tanks? Do you have a grill or something that uses propane?"

"Yes! There are two propane tanks out back by the grill."

"Okay," said Brooke. "That would give a fiery explosion. We'll still need something to set them off."

"I'll go to the garage," said Hans. He started that way, and the others decided to follow along. Strohm arrived ahead of him, opening one of the bays' arched carriage-style doors.

Strohm's garage was immaculate. The four-bay garage was clean, air-conditioned, and organized. The limousine was parked at one end, ever ready for service. A pair of luxury all-terrain-vehicles were parked next to it. A stainless-steel workbench spanned a quarter of the back wall, complete with tool drawers and a cabinet housing cleaning products. In the corner was a red five-gallon container.

"There," Strohm pointed, and Hans retrieved the plastic container.

"It feels full," said Hans.

"Good. Take it to the front porch."

Next, Strohm went through the house and out to the back patio. Chance went with him to the Kalamazoo grill. Strohm pulled two propane tanks from the storage cabinet, handing one to Chance. They brought the tanks inside and carried them to the front porch.

"All right," said Chance. "Now we need to plan this out. Step by step. We'll have one shot at doing this, so let's figure out how to execute it."

Stuart nodded. "That's right. We won't have much time in there. So how do we do this?"

"Um, we need a distraction," said Brooke. "Like, we can throw something in a far corner, let Boris go after it, and then toss in the gas and light it."

Strohm was sold. "Sounds perfect."

"What's our distraction?" Brandi said.

Everyone shrugged.

"Do we have a ham, or beef roast, or something like that?" Stuart asked. "It should be some kind of food."

"Uh, I'm not sure," said Strohm. "Let's take a look."

He went to his kitchen to search for anything they could use. Nothing in the freezer would do them any good; the bait had to have the scent of food. "Antoine!" he called.

The portly chef appeared a moment later. "Yes, sir?"

"Do we have any big meat?"

"Meat? What kind of—"

"Any! Like a ham, or, um—"

"There's a standing rib roast in the smoker for this evening's prime rib."

The billionaire's eyes lit up. "Perfect! Bring it to me!"

The chef seemed offended. "Now?"

"Right now! We need it for something."

"But, sir—"

"Now!"

Antoine hurried away to the electric smoker. He came back a minute later with an aromatic chunk of beef and rib bones.

"Yes!" said Strohm. "Thank you, Antoine." He and his crew left the kitchen, leaving the chef alone in bewilderment.

Carrying the roast, along with the gas container and propane tanks, the crew walked the hundred yards to the laboratory. Strohm stood ready at the keypad, his associates huddled around him.

"Okay," he said. "Here's what we're gonna do. Open the valves on those propane tanks when I say, all the way, and get that gas can open and ready to pour. And start pouring as you go in; we'll need to light the trail like a fuse. Chance, do you have your lighter?"

Chance pulled it from his pocket and struck the flint to test it. "Yep."

"Once I open the door," said Strohm, "we're going to toss the meat as far as we can. Then, when we see Boris go after it, we run in there and toss the leaking propane in. Hans, you'll bring and spill the gas as you go from here to where the tanks are, and drop it right there with them. Then everybody hurry back here, we light it, shut the door, and run like hell."

"Sounds good," Chance said.

Strohm then looked at each team member. "Are we ready?"

Everybody nodded, whether they were truly ready for this or not.

"All right, then." He took a deep breath and started punching in the access code. "Open the valves now…five…four…three…two…one!"

Strohm whipped the door open as soon as the latch disengaged, and he hurled the rib roast all the way to the far wall. It slapped against the wall and fell with a *smack* on the cement floor.

From out of nowhere, Boris appeared and charged straight for it.

The propane tanks were thrown in, and they bounded into the center of the lab, spewing invisible gas.

The creature took note of the tanks, then returned its attention to the meat. It started devouring the roast with a blur of furious teeth.

Hans rushed in with the plastic container, intentionally spilling a trail of gasoline as he went. He lobbed it near the hissing propane tanks, where it bounced and splashed.

There was a sudden flurry of movement. Fifty, maybe sixty, little creatures scampered out from behind the piranha tank. The eight-legged monsters were already a quarter of the size of Boris.

"Jesus Christ!" Stuart exclaimed. "They've already hatched!"

Before Hans could turn to see them, they swarmed him. Tiny legs scuttled up his pants. He immediately felt the pressure of multiple bites being taken out of his legs and torso.

Brandi's hands flew to her mouth. "OhmyGod!"

Shrieking, Hans frantically tried brushing them off. It was futile. The army of tiny teeth was frighteningly effective. So many bites, so quickly, so relentless. His body was running red with blood as he was being eaten alive. Hans felt flush with panic; he was going to pass out. He fell to the floor, and the little army finished him off.

"Light it! Light it!" screamed Strohm.

Chance darted to the edge of the spilled fuel. With a shaky hand, he flicked his lighter. He felt the hot flash as the gasoline ignited with a *whoosh* and sped to the tanks. Chance scrambled to the doorway.

Strohm slammed the door shut. "Run!"

The group fled across the yard, away from the concrete structure. They heard a loud concussion from within. Instinctively, they turned to make sure the building had remained intact. A few cracks were created, but the reinforced concrete held up.

"Yes!" said Brooke. Her tone was a combination of triumph and relief.

"Holyshit, holyshit," Stuart gushed. "That was crazy."

Chance took Brooke in his arms and kissed the top of her head as he held her. "Thank God," he sighed.

The group stood there for a while, just watching. Black smoke had made its way through an air vent on the roof.

That's a good thing, thought Chance. *The fire is raging in there.*

Suddenly, Stuart tensed. "Whoa, look! Look!"

The rest of the group saw it. Dozens of the deadly hatchlings were spilling out from beneath the cap on the roof vent.

CHAPTER 20

"No-no-no!" Brandi cried.

The group stared incredulously. They couldn't believe the creatures found a way out of the deathtrap.

"What the hell do we do now?" said Strohm.

"I—I don't know," Brooke replied. "But they're not contained anymore."

"Maybe we can lure them back to the house," said Chance.

Brandi's eyes were panicked. "Why would we do that?"

"We can't let them get away from here and spread throughout the area," he replied. "God only knows how many people they would kill if they got to the populated areas."

"We *have* to kill them," said Brooke. "But how?"

"I have several shotguns," Strohm suggested, "that I keep for skeet shooting."

"Let's go get 'em!" said Stuart.

He and Strohm ran to the house while the others watched the hatchlings collect atop the roof. Strohm led him into the study, and to the fancy gun case. They stuffed as many shells as they could in their pockets, readied the weapons, and hurried back outside.

"Hurry!" Brandi said. "They're starting to come down the wall!"

Chance saw the men carrying two Krieghoff K-80 sporting shotguns. "Those're some serious guns there," he noted.

"You shoot?" asked Strohm.

"Yeah."

Stuart handed over the one he was holding. "Here, then. I've never shot one."

"Gotcha." Chance gripped the over/under shotgun and checked to see that it was loaded. He then raised it and took aim at one of the many small targets climbing down the building. He squeezed the trigger.

The blast hit three of the beasts. They fell to the ground, fatally wounded.

"Yes!" said Stuart. "I'll keep feeding you shells when you need them!"

Strohm aimed and took a shot. Two more were hit; one of them stayed pasted to the wall.

The shooters stepped forward, getting closer to their oncoming targets while they fired. Fifty of the creatures were dribbling down the side of the building. It seemed like a hundred.

Brandi cringed as they got nearer to the ground. *"Get 'em, get 'em!"*

The groundskeeper came running, having heard the gunshots and yelling. "Sir! What is going on?"

"Javier," Strohm directed, "go to the house! Get Stephen, Marta and Antoine, and lock yourselves inside a secure place somewhere!"

Javier took one look at the monsters on the wall. *"Santa mierda!"* He scrambled to the house to do what he was told.

The hatchlings had reached the ground. There was no doubt of their collective will to attack the humans in their sight. They hustled directly toward them.

Strohm's security team—all three of them—had responded to the gunshots as well. It took them a few seconds to comprehend what was happening. Then, after a moment of shock from seeing the clutter of monsters, they pulled their sidearms and began shooting alongside the shotguns.

Stuart fed shells to Chance as needed, and Brooke assisted Strohm with his reloading. They kept firing at the approaching mass. Their blasts were hitting a small percentage of the animals.

But then the mass broke apart. Somehow, the creatures communicated and spread out in a thinner blanket. They weaved a little as they scuttled across the ground as well, making them harder to hit.

The shooters started stepping backward, attempting to keep more distance from the monsters. They continued firing their shotguns and Sig Sauer pistols. The shots were hitting some, but not nearly enough. There were just too many of them.

"We're gonna run out of ammo," Strohm declared. "We need to think of something else."

"What else do you have at the house?" asked Brandi.

"Nothing, weapon-wise. Just the comforts of home."

"What about electricity?" Brooke wondered. "Maybe we could find a way to trap and electrocute them."

"Maybe," Strohm said, having difficulty splitting his attention between the conversation and the approaching beasts.

One of the security team members decided he would have better luck if he got up close. Seeing him advance, the other two went with him. They got ten feet away and squeezed their triggers.

The targets were easier to hit up close. But despite the men's attempts to keep some distance, the creatures surprised them by speeding up and closing in on them from three sides.

Realizing the peril, the men tried to fall back. But it was too late. They were overtaken with savage, rapid teeth in numbers too large to combat with their hands. The men screamed and ran around.

One of them tried dropping and rolling, hoping that would help shed them. The ground was quickly littered with blood. The men were dead in less than a minute.

"I'm out!" Chance announced, after shooting his last shell.

Strohm fired two more times, and then he was out of ammo too. "Everyone! To the house!"

The group ran to Strohm's front porch. They hurried inside the house. Strohm shut the oak door and instinctively engaged the deadbolt.

"They'll be here in a few minutes," panted Stuart. "What do we do?"

"What could we use to electrocute them?" Brooke asked.

Brandi raised an eyebrow. "Electrocute?"

"Yeah. I can't think of any other means at our disposal."

"There's probably a two-hundred-forty-volt line going to the hot tub," said Chance. "Maybe we could use that?"

"The pool!" Brooke blurted. "If we could lure them in the water, we could electrocute them by running current into the pool."

Strohm nodded. "Yes, good! How would we lure them into the water, though?"

"I don't know," said Brooke. She looked out the patio window and noticed a floating lounger. "Is that made of rubber?"

Strohm followed her eyes and saw the lounger. "Yes, it is. Why?"

"Somebody could go out on that and be the bait."

"Whoa," said Stuart. "And be electrocuted to death?"

"I get it," said Brandi. "The rubber is an insulator, not a conductor. You'd be safe inside."

"What do you mean 'you'?" Stuart scoffed. "I'm not going out on that."

Strohm knew this could work. "You're right. Whoever goes on the floater would be shielded from the electricity."

Brooke nodded confidently. "Exactly."

The billionaire took a long breath. None of them should be the bait. They wouldn't be in this position if it weren't for his greedy ambition to accept the project in the first place. "I'll do it," he said.

The rest of the group was surprised by his volunteering, but they certainly weren't going to argue with him.

The sound of nibbling was heard at the front door. Hearing so many teeth gnawing away at the oak was chilling.

"They're here!" said Brandi.

"It won't take them long to chew through that wood," said Chance.

"Out back," Strohm directed. "We have to work fast."

They rushed to the back patio. When they were out, they slid the glass door shut.

"Back here," said Strohm, as he led them around the maintenance shed to the breaker box. He opened the panel and found the breaker for the hot tub. He switched it off. "One of you will have to flip this on once the animals are in the water," he stated.

Then Strohm rummaged through the maintenance shed for something to cut the wires. He found a gardening hatchet. *Perfect*, he grinned. He took it, ran to the hot tub, and chopped away at the power line. After three whacks, it was severed.

"All right," said Chance. "Let's get this in the pool." He grabbed the cable, yanking it away from the edge of the patio and pulling it to the poolside. Once he had moved enough of it, he dropped the exposed wires into the water.

The creatures had eaten through the front door and were now inside the house. Seeing movement on the patio, they scuttled to the sliding glass door.

Brandi jumped at the sound of the beasts butting the glass.

"Okay," Strohm said. "This is it, team." He dragged the inflated lounger to the edge of the pool. He lowered himself onto it, and then pushed off the edge and began drifting to the middle of the pool. "Get out of sight," he directed. "They must only see me, so that they'll all come for me."

"Someone has to open the door," said Stuart.

Chance spotted a landscaping brick, and he picked it up. "I got it."

The group went around the shed to hide.

Chance looked at Strohm. "Ready?"

Strohm took a deep breath. "Ready."

Brooke reached for the breaker and kept her fingers on it. "Ready," she said.

Chance took a few steps away, getting a better angle of the sliding door. Dozens of the fierce creatures were seen clamoring over each other trying to breach the glass. Chance cocked his arm back, hurled the brick at the patio door, and ducked back behind the shed.

The door shattered. A pile of creatures and glass spilled out onto the patio.

"Over here!" yelled Strohm, waving his arms to lure them. "Come get me!"

The beasts crowded to the water's edge. The sight of prey on the rubber lounger extinguished any uncertainty they had about the water. Their savage instinct to attack took over. They jumped into the pool and moved their legs spastically to swim toward Strohm.

Strohm's pulse was rising with fear and adrenaline. "That's it! Come on!"

Brooke leaned her head out to watch. She was ready to hit the switch, but not until every single one of them was in the water.

They were working their way through the water, getting close. Strohm felt panic, but he knew it wasn't time yet. He kept his eyes on the creatures that were still waiting for their turns to get into the pool. Each second felt like an eternity to Strohm.

Two of the animals had already reached the floating lounger. Strohm grit his teeth. Finally, after the last beast had entered the water, it was time.

"Now!" Strohm yelled. "Turn it on!"

Brooke thumbed the switch of the double breaker and flicked it on.

Current was released, charging the chemicals and minerals in the water. Electricity surged through the entire pool.

The creatures were gripped by the current. Their bodies clenched. They fought to keep moving, their brains pushing spasms to the muscle tissue.

The two that had reached the lounger managed to bite the rubber and tear a hole. The floater began to deflate rapidly.

"Nononono!" Strohm burbled, realizing he was about to sink into the electrified pool.

Some of the beasts gave in to the amperage. Paralysis took them, and they sank to drown.

Strohm tensed, his heart racing. His collapsing lounger was almost flat. "Shut it off!" he cried.

"Not yet," said Chance. "Some of them are still fighting, still alive."

Brooke's fingers trembled on the switch.

Strohm's weight submerged the deflated lounger. Water covered him, and he instantly felt his body clenching from the electricity.

"N—n— n—!"

The sight was horrific for the group to see. "Shut it off!" screamed Brandi, watching Strohm seize.

Brooke shook her head, still seeing some of the animals convulsing on the surface.

"We're gonna kill him!"

"Not until they're all dead!" Brooke insisted.

"This is our only chance to kill them," admitted Stuart. "We *have* to wait until they're dead."

The group studied the activity in the pool. Strohm went under. This was an awful situation, but deep down, they all knew they had to make sure every last creature was killed. Even if it meant Strohm didn't survive the ordeal.

Once the last creature had surrendered to its fate and disappeared beneath the surface, Brooke flipped the switch off.

The group trotted to the edge of the pool and surveyed the depths. Twenty-seven creatures lay dead at the bottom. Strohm's body was down there as well, right in the middle of the mass. It was a ghastly sight.

"Oh God, he's dead," sobbed Brandi.

Stuart draped his arms around her and held her.

"Jesus," said Chance. "That was…" He couldn't find the words to finish his statement.

Brooke felt like crying. But she couldn't. All she could do was gaze into the pool and watch the lifeless tarantula legs sway in the water's gentle current.

CHAPTER 21

Media coverage swarmed the edge of the estate. They were desperate to get information about why an ambulance was at Felix Strohm's home, and why the Army had secured the area and was keeping everyone out.

Colonel Pascavage was on site. He stood on the front lawn with the group of researchers, interviewing them to learn what had happened. Army paramedics carried a stretcher to the ambulance, and the group watched. Their eyes followed the lifeless form under the white cover.

"All right," said Pascavage, "let's go over it one more time."

The young scientists had discussed what to say before they'd called the authorities. They agreed that it would be in everybody's best interests to omit the truth about how long they had let the electricity flow into the pool. Instead, they would testify that they shut the breaker off as soon as they noticed Strohm had entered the water, but sadly, it was too late. That would satisfy the authorities.

"Just like we said, sir," Chance responded. "The animals could not be contained. In order to control the situation as much as we could, we lured them to the house."

"So they wouldn't get out among the public," said Stuart.

"Yes. They could've killed hundreds of people if they made it off the property."

The colonel nodded his acknowledgement of that fact.

"If we didn't find a way to kill them," Chance continued, "they would've killed us. They were relentless. My God, they ate their way in through the front door trying to get to us!"

"And that's when you went to the pool area?"

"Yes. We knew our only shot at stopping them was to electrify the pool and get them to go in."

The colonel grunted. "I find it hard to believe that Mr. Strohm would volunteer to be the bait."

"But he did," Brooke affirmed. "Our plan was that he would be safe inside the rubber floater."

"And the plan worked, until the floater popped?"

Chance nodded. "Nobody expected they would get that close to him before we could flip the switch."

"But when they did, you cut the power?"

"As soon as we noticed he'd gone in the water," said Brooke. "But it was already too late." She felt jittery not telling the truth, but she knew they'd done the right thing. As tragic as Strohm's death was, the threat had to be destroyed.

Pascavage eyed each scientist, and they returned his glance with an affirming nod.

"Mr. Strohm took the risk being the bait to save us," said Chance. "He was a great man."

The colonel conceded. "A damn shame."

"Yes, sir," the others concurred.

"What about the research? Can it be continued?"

Whether it could or not, nobody in the group wanted any more part of this nightmare.

"I don't think so," said Stuart. "There's just no way to control an animal like that. Despite our best efforts, they repeatedly managed to find a way to escape and multiply. I'm sorry, sir, but the project has failed."

"We tried," said Chance. "We gave a brilliant effort and made some progresses, but in the end, nature has a limit to its cooperation."

Pascavage grunted again.

"So…," Brandi said, "are we free to go?"

The Army colonel had no hold over the scientists. They had agreed to work for Strohm, not the Army.

"Yes, I think so," said Pascavage. "Just keep in mind that you're bound to confidentiality about your work for the Department of Defense. Forever. I take it that's clear for each of you?"

"Yes, sir," they replied solemnly.

"All right. I'll need all of you to sign some more paperwork for me, but you're clear to go after that."

The group had no problem with that. They walked with the colonel to wrap things up.

Brooke turned to Chance while they moved across the lawn. "What are you going to do after this?"

He shrugged. "I really have no idea. You?"

"Me neither."

"At least we have enough money from this to take some time to figure out what each of us is going to do next."

Brooke's eyes locked with his. "What do you say we figure it out together?"

Chance smiled warmly. "I'd have to say that's a totally terrific plan."

The End

AUTHOR'S NOTE

I want to thank you for reading this crazy little nightmare. I truly hope you enjoyed my homage to mutant creature features. Special thanks to Angela Yuriko Smith, who came up with the name Pirantulas before I did, but gave her blessing for me to release my own story under the same name.

As always, be safe, be kind, and be well.

Check out other great

Cryptid Novels!

P.K. Hawkins

THE CRYPTID FILES

Fresh out of the academy with top marks, Agent Bradley Tennyson is expecting to have the pick of cases and investigations throughout the country. So he's shocked when instead he is assigned as the new partner to "The Crag," an agent well past his prime. He thinks the assignment is a punishment. It's anything but. Agent George Crag has been doing this job for far longer than most, and he knows what skeletons his bosses have in the closet and where the bodies are buried. He has pretty much free reign to pick his cases, and he knows exactly which one he wants to use to break in his new young partner: the disappearance and murder of a couple of college kids in a remote mountain town. Tennyson doesn't realize it, but Crag is about to introduce him to a world he never believed existed: The Cryptid Files, a world of strange monsters roaming in the night. Because these murders have been going on for a long time, and evidence is mounting that the murderer may just in fact be the legendary Bigfoot.

Gerry Griffiths

DOWN FROM BEAST MOUNTAIN

A beast with a grudge has come down from the mountain to terrorize the townsfolk of Porterville. The once sleepy town is suddenly wide awake. Sheriff Abel McGuire and game warden Grant Tanner frantically investigate one brutal slaying after another as they follow the blood trail they hope will eventually lead to the monstrous killer. But they better hurry and stop the carnage before the census taker has to come out and change the population sign on the edge of town to ZERO.

SEVERED**PRESS**

Check out other great
Cryptid Novels!

Hunter Shea
THE DOVER DEMON

The Dover Demon is real...and it has returned. In 1977, Sam Brogna and his friends came upon a terrifying, alien creature on a deserted country road. What they witnessed was so bizarre, so chilling, they swore their silence. But their lives were changed forever. Decades later, the town of Dover has been hit by a massive blizzard. Sam's son, Nicky, is drawn to search for the infamous cryptid, only to disappear into the bowels of a secret underground lair. The Dover Demon is far deadlier than anyone could have believed. And there are many of them. Can Sam and his reunited friends rescue Nicky and battle a race of creatures so powerful, so sinister, that history itself has been shaped by their secretive presence? "THE DOVER DEMON is Shea's most delightful and insidiously terrifying monster yet." – Shotgun Logic Reviews "An excellent horror novel and a strong standout in the UFO and cryptid subgenres." –Hellnotes "Non-stop action awaits those brave enough to dive into the small town of Dover, and if you're lucky, you won't see the Demon himself!" – The Scary Reviews PRAISE FOR SWAMP MONSTER MASSACRE "B-horror movie fans rejoice, Hunter Shea is here to bring you the ultimate tale of terror!" – Horror Novel Reviews "A nonstop thrill ride! I couldn't put this book down." – Cedar Hollow Horror Reviews

Armand Rosamilia
THE BEAST

The end of summer, 1986. With only a few days left until the new school year, twins Jeremy and Jack Schaffer are on very different paths. Jeremy is the geek, playing Dungeons & Dragons with friends Kathleen and Randy, while Jack is the jock, getting into trouble with his buddies. And then everything changes when neighbor Mister Higgins is killed by a wild animal in his yard. Was it a bear? There's something big lurking in the woods behind their New Jersey home. Will the police be able to solve the murder before more Middletown residents are ripped apart?

Check out other great

Cryptid Novels!

Ian Faulkner
CRYPTID

Be careful what you look for. You might just find it.1996. A group of 14 students walked into the trackless virgin forests of Graham Island, British Columbia for a three-day hike. They were never seen again. 2019. An American TV crew retrace those students' steps to attempt to solve a 23-year-old mystery.A disparate collection of characters arrives on the island. But all is not as it seems. Two of them carry dark secrets. Terrible knowledge that will mean death for some – but a fighting chance of survival for others. In the hidden depths of the forests – man is on the menu. Some mysteries should remain unsolved...

Eric S. Brown
LOCH NESS HORROR

The Order of the Eternal Light, a secret organization have foretold the end of the human race. In order to save all humanity, agents of the Order must locate the Loch Ness Monster and obtain a sample of its blood for within in it is the key to stopping the apocalypse but finding the monster will be no easy task.